"Let's not pretend.... We both know exactly what kind of woman you are. You want money, and I am prepared to see you get a fair settlement."

His hands slid up her arms and tightened on her shoulders. His closeness, the masculine warmth of him tantalized her senses, even as anger at his misguided assumptions about her colored her cheeks. She glanced helplessly up into his hard face, unable to find a cutting response. His mouth descended and she waited for his kiss, but instead he continued talking.

"I can see you get a lot more if you like," he declared huskily. "I'm also quite prepared to take up where Paolo left off, and keep you as my mistress."

JACQUELINE BAIRD began writing as a hobby when her family objected to the smell of her oil painting, and immediately became hooked on the romance genre. She loves traveling and worked her way around the world from Europe to the Americas and Australia, returning to marry her teenage sweetheart. She lives in the north of England, in the county of her birth, and has two grown-up sons.

JACQUELINE BAIRD

Mistaken for a Mistress

Harlequin Books

TORONTO • NEW YORK • LONDON
AMSTERDAM • PARIS • SYDNEY • HAMBURG
STOCKHOLM • ATHENS • TOKYO • MILAN
MADRID • WARSAW • BUDAPEST • AUCKLAND

ISBN 0-373-11915-1

MISTAKEN FOR A MISTRESS

First North American Publication 1997.

Copyright © 1997 by Jacqueline Baird.

This edition published by arrangement with Harlequin Books S.A.

Printed in U.S.A.

CHAPTER ONE

To GO or not to go to Italy? That was the question. Marlene, her hand curved around a nasty weed, gave a vicious tug then paused dramatically, the weed half pulled out of the dry ground. To honour a dying man's last wish, or conveniently forget about it for her own peace of mind. She yanked the offending weed out completely, dropped it, then wiped her sweat-soaked brow with the back of her hand. She decided it was too hot to make a serious decision and instead collapsed flat on her back on the brown earth.

She gazed up through the fluttering canopy of bushy green leaves to the clear blue sky above and sighed. She loved the garden, and occasionally thoroughly enjoyed meeting the mixed bag of customers. The Johanson Herb garden attracted, but weeding between row upon row of raspberry bushes on a hot July afternoon was not usually her idea of fun. Today, though, for some reason she had needed the hard physical labour to take her mind off her more pressing problems. In the distance the low murmur of voices floated on the summer air, but it did not disturb her reverie because the garden was closed to visitors on Mondays.

Strictly speaking, she mused, raspberries could hardly be classed as herbs, but because her grandfather had planted them years ago neither Marlene nor her late mother, for that matter, had ever had the heart to uproot the things.

At the thought of her mother, Marlene's golden eyes shadowed with sorrow. Two years had passed since a drunken driver had mown her mother down, and the memory only served to remind her of a more recent tragedy, almost as painful. Twenty months after the death of her mother, Paolo Rossi, her mother's lover, father of her brother Paul and a good friend and mentor to Marlene, had died suddenly of a massive heart attack, in March of this year.

She grimaced at her morbid thoughts, then frowned, nibbling on her full bottom lip in nervous indecision. For more than two months now the letter from a London firm of solicitors acting on behalf of their Italian associate company had lain unanswered on the dressing table in her bedroom. She knew she was going to have to answer it soon. But how? That was the problem. Judging by the personal revelations Paolo had shared with her just before his death, and the remarks he had made about his family in Italy during the eight years Marlene had known him, she was not at all sure she should subject young Paul to their influence—even if a fortune in property was involved. There were more things of value in life than money, as she knew to her cost...

At that moment it dawned on Marlene that the distant voices were a heck of a lot closer, and by an amazing coincidence the language they were using was Italian. Or was it her imagination running riot? She stiffened and would have stood up, but something made her stop.

It was a woman's voice, shrill and rapid.

'Honestly, Rocco, for Papà to take a mistress who digs in the dirt for a living is unbelievable—and to actually give her a percentage of the company and a seat on the board is just too much. He must have known my mother, the Contessa, would be forced to recognise the bitch. It simply beggars belief. You have got to persuade the woman to sell her holdings for a few thousand pounds and to disappear with her bastard child.'

Marlene turned scarlet with embarrassment and anger at the callous comments. Having studied Italian and French as secondary subjects at university, she had understood every hate-filled word. That this creature should presume Marlene had been Paolo's mistress and mother of young Paul was bad enough, when it had been her mother and Paolo who had loved each other quite desperately and produced the darling little boy. But to call an innocent child a bastard even if technically it was true was beyond the pale...

Marlene guessed immediately who the woman was. It could only be the late Paolo Rossi's legitimate daughter. But she had more sense than to stand up and confront the spiteful female. 'Know thine enemy,' she murmured under her breath, and peered surreptitiously through the bushes.

A thin, fashionable, dark-haired woman of about her own age—twenty-six—was picking her way along the narrow path in stiletto-heeled white shoes. Dressed in a pink suit, obviously designer label, she clung to the arm of her companion—and what a companion!

Marlene's eyes widened in awe and a tingling sensation slid down her spine. She had limited experience with men but even she could recognise that he was a fabulous example of the male species. About six feet four of sheer masculine perfection. His cream pleated trousers clung lovingly to lean hips, and a cream-and-brown-patterned tailored shirt, open at the neck, revealed the beginnings of crisp black body hair and emphasised his broad chest. A soft cream matching sweater draped elegantly over incredibly wide shoulders completed the ensemble.

The whole outfit screamed Armani. But this man would have looked good in anything—or *nothing,* she thought with sinful erotic delight. The image forming in her brain of the man naked made her pulse race, and she swallowed hard, fighting down a sudden total body blush!

The man was a hunk. He had it all. The way he moved, the proud tilt of his head, even the sun catching the odd strand of silver in the longer than fashionable black hair declared to the world at large that here was a dynamic, powerful man—a man who would bow to no one, a man who was used to the best and would not settle for anything less.

Marlene suddenly shivered. A man, moreover, who looked vaguely familiar. Did she know him? He was rather like Julian, she realised, remembering her one and only disastrous love affair. Julian had been a ruthless devil, trying to use her love for him to further his career at the expense of hers, until she had found out and ditched him.

This man had the same predatory look about him, but even more so. Maybe that was why she'd thought she recognised him, why her mouth was dry and her heart was pounding as if she were a teenager with a surfeit of hormones.

No, she could not possibly know him, she told herself firmly, dismissing the notion with a faint shake of her head. As for her body's instant reaction to him, well, she had probably been in the sun too long. She rationalised her behaviour and, never one to shirk a confrontation, she decided to challenge the arrogant pair and put them straight about Paolo's relationship with her mother. Until she heard a deep, conciliatory voice responding to the woman.

'Don't worry, Caterina. Leave it all to me. I have dealt with her kind of low-life before. The woman will not be a problem for long, I promise.'

Low-life. Marlene was almost apoplectic! How dared the swine refer to her in that way? She took a deep breath and remembered some good advice from Paolo: 'Don't get mad, get even'. And in that second her mind was made up. She would have some fun with the pair, and take them down a peg or two in the process, before getting down to business. They deserved it.

Rolling onto her knees, she stood up, her back to the approaching couple, and, stretching to her full height of five feet nine, turned slowly. Acting for all she was worth, she feigned startled surprise at seeing two strangers in the garden. Pushing her tangled blonde hair from her face, then slowly rubbing mud-caked hands on the denim cut-offs that barely covered her hips, she stepped towards them.

'I'm sorry, sir, madam, but the garden is closed today.' Marlene concentrated her attention on the woman, searching for some trace of her beloved Paolo in the smooth features, but there was little resemblance. The eyes might have been the same, except where Paolo's had been rich chocolate-brown, twinkling with humour at life, this girl's were cold and hard.

'We do not buy. We...er...er—' The woman spoke in fractured English but the man interrupted.

'My companion does not speak very much English. Allow me to explain the reason for our intrusion, Miss Johanson. I can assure you it will be to your benefit.'

At the mention of her name Marlene was forced to confront the man. She had to tilt her head back to look up into his hard, autocratic face—unusual for her—and when she did her eyes widened in appalled recognition. She had seen him before. It had been at the lowest point of her life to date, and one she would never forget. In that instant she knew this man would never do anything for her benefit; the truth was quite the reverse. She could see it in his black eyes, in the flicker of grim animosity he could not quite disguise.

Unconsciously her gracefully arched eyebrows drew together in a concentrated frown, her mind spinning back to their last meeting. She had just been to the morgue to identify the shattered remains of her mother's body. Paolo had accompanied her, of course, but as he hadn't been technically a relation—although he had virtually lived with her mother for the past few years—he could not do the job for Marlene. But his support had been a great comfort, and later, when he'd insisted they must try to eat, she had accompanied him to a small French restaurant in the centre of London.

Both emotionally distraught, they had been idly pushing the food around their plates when the man who stood before her now had walked into the restaurant with a glamorous red-headed woman on his arm. Spotting Paolo, he had forced an introduction from him.

Paolo, completely distracted, had simply introduced Marlene as his friend, Miss Johanson, and had made it very obvious that he did not want to make polite conversation. Marlene, even in her distress, had registered the cynical contempt in the man's eyes when he had responded abruptly.

'Charmed, Miss Johanson,' he had said, and his low-voiced murmur, 'And no doubt expensive...' had not hurt her at the time, because all her pain had been concentrated on the loss of her mother.

Now, however, it was a different matter. She could not remember his name. but she knew his type. Her golden eyes clashed with black and she saw the self-same contempt as before. And this time she resolved to make the arrogant swine pay for his attitude.

'Explain away,' she finally responded casually. 'But I can't imagine we have anything to discuss.' And, fluttering her long eyelashes flirtatiously, she added, lying, 'I'm sure I would remember *you* if I had met you before.'

'We have met once, briefly, but your attention was concentrated on your companion at the time.' The hard mouth twisted cynically. 'It is not surprising you do not remember me. Allow me to introduce myself again. I am Rocco Andretti and this—' he smiled briefly at the small woman at his side '—this is Caterina Rossi, the daughter of Paolo Rossi—someone I believe you were extremely well acquainted with,' he said with thinly veiled disdain.

Marlene was left in no doubt as to his opinion of her and her relationship with the late Paolo, and she saw no reason to enlighten this stuck-up pair with the truth. Instead she merely looked blank and said, with the slightest shrug of her shoulders, 'Yes? So...' And she hid a secret smile as she registered the anger her casual response had ignited in the man's dark eyes.

'I'm sure you can guess why we are here. As I understand it, our London associates did write to you,' Rocco said curtly, 'but there seems to have been some delay or difficulty in your replying.'

'I was never much good at writing, I'm afraid.' Marlene excused her lapse with simpering false naïvety.

'So we gathered—hence our appearance here. We wish to reach some amicable agreement over Signor Rossi's will and the shares you hold in his company as soon as possible.'

Is that the royal 'we'? Marlene was tempted to snap back sarcastically, but common sense prevailed. Instead, ignoring the penetrating gaze of Rocco Andretti, and most of what he had said, she forced a smile to her lips and held out her hand to the other woman. After all, common human decency decreed that the woman was deserving of sympathy at the loss of her father, even if she did appear to be a grade A bitch.

'It is a pleasure to meet you, Caterina. Paolo was a lovely man—you must miss him greatly,' she murmured.

At the look of horror on Caterina's face Marlene glanced down at her very dirty extended hand, which Caterina had taken one look at and ignored. With a barely restrained grin, Marlene dropped her hand.

'You're right, of course—I am rather mucky. If you would like to follow me to the office...' Her gaze strayed to a tumbledown shed in one corner of the huge walled garden and an imp of mischief lit her wide golden eyes before she added, 'I'll wash my hands and we can talk there.'

Caterina turned to Rocco and burst into a torrent of Italian. 'My God, Rocco. Look at the woman. She can't be any more than a few years older than me, and so coarse—nothing more than a peasant. How could Papà?'

A few years older! In her dreams, Marlene thought, and had to fight the angry retort that sprang to her lips. She plastered a dumb, questioning smile on her lovely face and forced herself to stand still as Andretti's dark eyes swept her briefly clad body with slow and blatant masculine appraisal, taking in her flushed face, the tumble of thick blonde hair, her skimpy white cropped top, bare midriff and brief cut-offs, travelling down her long, long legs and then back to her face. And all the time he spoke in soft Italian.

'Enough, Caterina. She looks like a dumb blonde country yokel, but even so she might understand some of what we say. After all, she was your father's mistress for eight years—perhaps some of the pillow-talk rubbed off, if nothing else. We can't afford to take any chances.' ·

And when his eyes finally met Marlene's he smiled, a totally false twist of his lips, and raised his voice. *'Scusi, signorina, parla italiano?'*

Her face rosy with anger, which she hoped he would put down to embarrassment, not by a flicker of an eyelash did Marlene betray that she understood every word. Instead she gestured with her hand. 'The office shed is down here—if you've finished your chat?' She smiled questioningly back at the pair of them and almost chuckled as she saw the relieved glance that passed between them.

'Lead on, Miss Johanson. We are completely at your disposal,' Rocco said blandly. 'I'm sure you are as anxious as we are to get this little matter settled.'

Making no response—she could not, she was so incensed—she spun on her heel and strode along the narrow pebbled path. 'Little matter' indeed! she fumed. A twenty-four per cent share in a multi-million-pound business empire and a seat on the board of directors was hardly 'little' by anyone's standards. Never mind the added complication of a villa in Amalfi for young Paul, if she decided to take him there.

This couple obviously thought she was a complete idiot—a dead man's ex-mistress to be bought off with a few pounds. They had callously insulted her—and Paolo and her late mother too, for that matter. Well, they were in for a very rude awakening, Marlene vowed silently. If they had been even faintly polite, faintly compassionate about the recent death of a lovely man, she would have invited them to the house and listened to what they had to say. But as it was Ned's old shed was more than good enough for the arrogant, conceited jerks.

Reaching the shed, she opened the door, a spark of devilment in her eyes. The shed was more of a lean-to, built against the wall of the magnificent walled garden that was the home of The Johanson Herb Garden. She crossed the confined space, pushing past a battered old wooden chair and table so she could reach the cracked pottery sink set against the wall behind them. She turned on the rusty tap and proceeded to wash her filthy hands with a tiny sliver of old soap, taking her time about it.

Decades ago, as a young man, her grandfather had escaped during the Second World War from German-occupied Holland to England. He had found employment as a gardener at a stately home set in acres of rolling countryside in Sussex. The lady of the house, a Mrs Barker-Smythe, lost her son in the war and later, in the fifties, her husband. Meanwhile Grandpa Johanson had met and married an English girl and taken up residence in the old coach house alongside the stables and attached to the back of the walled garden. Marlene's mother had been born in the house and had delighted in telling her daughter the story.

Apparently Mrs Barker-Smythe had begun to find money in short supply, and with no family left had reached an agreement with Grandpa Johanson. She'd given him a hundred-year lease on the coach house and walled garden on the estate, to develop it into a money-making market garden, with two conditions. One, that he planted a rose garden in front of the massive iron gates set in the wall between the big house and the garden, so her view would not be spoilt by rows of vegetables, and secondly that he and his wife would look after Mrs Barker-Smythe for nothing until her death.

The shed had been the original office, donkey's years ago. Now there was a very smart one in the converted stableblock, along with a retail outlet and coffee-shop. Ned oversaw the actual planting, and the manager, John Watson, with a permanent staff of six, plus casual workers at the busiest times, made sure that both the wholesale and the retail side of the business ran smoothly.

After the death of her grandfather, when Marlene was still a baby, her mother had inherited the place, but with the influx of fruit and vegetables from all over the world becoming more and more common, and so reducing the profit on home-produced stock grown on a small scale, the business had been in difficulty by the time her own father had died when she was only three.

Marlene barely remembered him, but her mother had kept his memory alive with photographs and stories of when they were young. He had been a good man. A cousin from Marlene's grandfather's side of the family before he was a husband, and her mother had often joked about how her name had never changed when she had married.

Left with a three-year-old daughter to take care of, and no other form of income, her mother had decided to concentrate on herbs, with the assumption that the work would be slightly less strenuous and that herbs were going to be the crop of the future. Her hunch had proved correct. It was now a very profitable business. One, moreover, that Marlene had very little to do with. Her expertise was in a completely different field.

A discreet cough broke Marlene's train of thought. She shook her head to dismiss the memories and, straightening up, turned off the tap. She reached up to take a piece of torn towel from a nail on the wall and dried her hands. She saw no reason to tell the two people behind her the truth. Let them think she was an empty-headed bimbo—it should be interesting!

'Sorry about this, but the muck does take a lot of shifting—especially from under the fingernails, I find,' she said blithely, turning around to face her visitors while dropping the scrap of towel strategically over the ancient order papers on the table, in case the shrewd Andretti saw them.

'I would ask you both to sit down, but as you see there is only one chair. We don't go much for office furniture.'

At that precise moment a huge spider fell from the rafters, suspended on a silken thread. Highlighted by a ray of sun slanting through the door, it spun inches from Caterina's face like a golden tarantula.

A high-pitched scream rent the air and a swirl of pink shot out of the door and off up the pebbled path as fast as white stilettos would allow.

Marlene spluttered, and with a hand to her mouth she tried to disguise her amusement with a fit of coughing. Not very successfully...

'You don't go much for good manners either, it would seem,' Rocco Andretti said bitingly, and, catching her by the arm, he hauled her hard against his tall body.

Too astonished to resist, Marlene looked up, all amusement vanishing at the sight of the venom she recognised in his narrowed black eyes.

'You dare to laugh at Caterina when you are not fit to kiss the feet of a lady like her, you gold-digging little whore. Be warned, it is me you have to deal with now, and I am nothing like the gullible old fool Paolo was. It takes more than a luscious body, a beautiful face and fluttering eyelashes to fool me. Try playing games with me, and I will make you sorry you were ever born—and that is a promise, Miss Johanson.'

It sounded more like a threat than a promise, Marlene thought cynically, while feeling oddly flattered that he had called her beautiful. Which just shows what a fool I am, she said to herself silently. The knives were out, she realised, and this man would carve her into little pieces given half a chance. But she refused to be intimidated. Four years as a foreign exchange dealer with a large firm of stockbrokers had taught her how to hold her own with any man.

'Worried, Miss Johanson?' the mocking voice drawled near her ear. 'You should be.'

It was the edge of triumph in his tone that really angered Marlene, and, ignoring the shiver of pleasure his breath against her cheek aroused, she finally asked the question she should have asked ten minutes ago.

'And who exactly are you, Signor Andretti?' she prompted insinuatingly, boldly holding his gaze. 'The immaculate Caterina's lover? Or perhaps her financial adviser, hoping to line your own pockets? Just who gave you the right to interfere in my affairs?' She felt his long fingers tighten angrily on her bare skin, and a jolt of something very like electricity shot up her arm, making her catch her breath in surprise.

'I would not touch your "affairs" with a barge-boat,' he drawled, the double meaning obvious.

Marlene's lips twitched slightly at the word 'boat'. It was the first and only sign of weakness in his otherwise perfect English. But he made no mistake in the threat that followed.

'My father's law firm is responsible for administering Signor Rossi's estate. Paolo was clever, signing over the stock to you but still administering it himself. No one knew he was voting his mistress's shares along with his own. But he is not around to protect you any more. The Contessa and Caterina are long-time family friends, and anything I can do to stop you getting your grubby little hands on any more of his assets I will.'

So Signor Andretti was Paolo's lawyer, Marlene realised with a sinking heart. And he was obviously more loyal to the female members of the Rossi family than he was to the late Paolo Rossi. The shares he was talking about had been put in her mother's name years ago by Paolo, and when her mother had died the shares had passed to Marlene.

She stared up into his dark face. 'For a lawyer you're not too bright. I already have the shares,' she reminded him sarcastically, at the same time fighting to ignore the primitive attraction simply being so close to him aroused in her.

'Women like you should not be allowed to profit at the expense of legitimate family simply by spreading their legs,' Rocco declared scathingly.

Shocked rigid by the insult, Marlene felt her golden eyes widen at the look of cold determination on his hard face, and she knew she should have answered the letter from the English law firm when she'd had the chance, and so avoided this confrontation with a highly volatile Latin...

She dropped her gaze to the lips that were mouthing the threats. He had a nice mouth, a sensuous mouth—and what was that enticing scent? The lingering trace of some masculine cologne, or simply the man? she wondered. God! What was she thinking of? She jerked her arm out of his grasp, horrified at the erotic turn her mind had taken. She needed to get out of the shed, out of this man's presence—and quick.

'*Rocco, caro.*' A tremulous voice broke the tense silence and a second later Marlene was watching

Andretti's broad back as he strode up the garden to the waiting Caterina.

Marlene hesitated for a moment in an attempt to regain her equilibrium and control of the situation. Perhaps Andretti was right. It had been stupid to play games with the couple, and she would have to be even more stupid to continue doing so having felt the full force of Rocco's powerful personality.

After all, it had been Paolo's one and only request of her in eight years. He had known he had not long to live well before the massive heart attack that had finally killed him. They had spent his last few weeks together, mostly in his London apartment, and it was then he had revealed to Marlene his worry that someone on the board of his multinational electronics firm was deliberately blackening the good name of Rossi. Consequently the share price was dropping dramatically for no real reason.

He had asked her to investigate for him, and she had half promised that she would go to Italy and try to find out what was going on, not wishing to upset him when he was so ill. It was only after he was dead that she had discovered a very personal letter from him, reminding her of her promise and a few other things.

Marlene sighed deeply, and reluctantly followed after her visitors, finally deciding to tell the truth, or at least some of it. She did not know if Rocco and Caterina were mixed up in the dodgy business in Italy, and until she did she would keep quiet on that front. But as for the rest, she was an intelligent, highly educated young woman. She spoke Italian and French, and she was also exceptionally successful, having made her first million by the tender age of twenty-four. It would do the arrogant Andretti no harm to realise she was a more than capable adversary. She had been taught by the best . . .

Rocco and Caterina were talking heatedly, their backs to her, and did not hear her approach. Marlene was a few feet away, about to make her presence known, when all her good intentions flew out of the window as she overheard their conversation yet again.

'All right. All right, Caterina, have it your way. Actually, having met the woman again, I am inclined to agree with you. I called her a whore and a gold-digger and she made no attempt to deny it. Even she can't be so dense as to put up with an insult like that unless it's true. We will try to buy her shares first. As for the rest, I believe the boy is young enough to be controlled. All we have to do is prove she is an unfit mother.'

'I knew you would see it my way, *caro.* I saw the way she looked at you in that hovel that passes for an office, Rocco. If we can't find an ex-lover here to blacken her name, a man of your undoubted skill could easily seduce her and expose her for the slut she is. She'll be putty in your hands.' And Caterina's own hand slid suggestively down his chest as she smiled up at him.

Her smile was reciprocated by the slow, knowing curl of Rocco's sensuous mouth as he placed his hand over Caterina's and casually removed it from his chest. 'I'm flattered by your faith in me,' and I think I might just be able to force myself to seduce her.'

In that moment Marlene came as near to exploding with rage as she ever had in her whole life. It was only with a superhuman effort of will that she made herself cover the few paces that separated them, and, ignoring Rocco completely, she looked directly at Caterina.

'I'm so sorry about the spider—I do hope you're all right. You must be suffering from shock. How awful for you.' She knew she was babbling but it stopped her having to face the hateful man, and, grabbing Caterina's arm, she urged her forward. 'Come along to the house. Hot, sweet tea is what you need.'

In reality what the arrogant, conniving couple needed was a swift kick in the butt and expulsion from the premises, Marlene silently fumed. They thought she was immoral and that Paul was her son, and they were quite prepared to do anything to get the boy away from her and under their control... They were in for a very rude awakening—but not yet, she vowed...

CHAPTER TWO

'MAR, Mar—I'm back.' The appearance of a small boy running across the garden stopped the Italian couple in their tracks.

But Marlene didn't notice as she let go of Caterina's arm and dashed off on a diagonal path to meet young Paul. Swooping down, she picked him up and swung him high in the air. 'Hello, darling,' she cried happily, and nuzzled the soft black curls of his head before lowering him to his feet and asking, 'How was playschool today? You were a good boy, I hope.'

Straightening up, she waved to her friend Jean who was standing at the entrance door set in the twelve-foot-high wall. They ran a rota to transport the children the ten miles to pre-school. Today had been Jean's turn. 'Thanks, Jean,' Marlene called. 'See you in the morning.'

The young mother grinned and shouted back, 'Thank God my stint is over for a couple of days. That Paul of yours takes more controlling than all the rest put together—and boy, can he *talk*.'

Marlene waved again and watched her friend leave, glad that Jean had referred to Paul as hers. It might help to prolong the belief of the other two in her motherhood. But she need not have worried. When she looked down for Paul she discovered that he was heading for the two visitors, a determined expression on his chubby face.

She shot after him in time to hear him demand inquisitively, 'Who are you? Why you here? Today is my Mar's holiday.'

The fact that he called her Mar reinforced the belief that she was his mother. A tender smile curved Marlene's

21

wide mouth. Paul sounded so like his father—macho-male and very protective. It was uncanny in a child not yet four years old. She reached down and rumpled his dark curls with a gentle hand.

'It's all right, Paul, they're...' she hesitated for a second '...friends.' And, looking across at Caterina and Rocco, she almost chuckled out loud at the look of distaste on the other woman's face.

Rocco glanced down at the child, then straight at Marlene. 'So this boy is your son?' he demanded, with evident disgust darkening his hard face.

A surge of anger almost made Marlene blurt out the truth, but she knew it would do neither Paul nor herself any good to lose control in front of this astute man. Her mind working fast, she realised it was to her advantage to let them think she was Paul's mother, and for once she blessed her young brother's habit of shortening her name to Mar.

'The boy is your son?' Rocco Andretti repeated his question curtly.

Equally curtly Marlene responded, not lying exactly—except perhaps by omission. 'The boy has a name. Paul—named after his father, Paolo Rossi—and I would thank you to use it. He also has ears,' she warned him sharply. Any discussion of Paul's parentage was not going to take place in front of him, if she could prevent it.

Paul, bored by even a minute's inactivity, chose that moment to acknowledge Caterina. 'You are a pretty pink lady, but not as big as Mar.'

'Dio grazie,' Caterina murmured insultingly.

But Rocco cut in before Marlene could retaliate. 'Hello, young man. Paul, is it?'

Marlene's eyes widened in astonishment as Rocco dropped to his haunches and smiled at the little boy. The smile transformed his harsh features into charming, almost boyish beauty, with just a hint of mischief and a subtle male bonding in his gleaming dark eyes.

He was really quite endearing, she thought, her own eyes lingering with rapt fascination on his tanned face. He was the most exquisite man she had ever seen, and for a long moment she simply stared, until Rocco flicked a glance her way, with a knowing, purely male grin twisting his sensuous mouth. Suddenly remembering he was the enemy, she hastily lowered her eyes from his too attractive face—but that was a mistake.

The fabric of his trousers was pulled tight across his knees and clung to his muscular thighs like a second skin, filling her head with wildly erotic thoughts that brought hot colour to her cheeks. She shook her head in confusion and, pushing back her hair from her brow, looked over the top of the two males at Caterina. The flash of sheer hatred in the other woman's eyes brought her back to her senses with a jolt. Just in time to tune in to the conversation going on at her feet.

Rocco's deep, melodious voice, his almost perfect command of English, had Paul enthralled. 'I knew your father very well, and you look very like him. I would have recognised you anywhere, Paul. I hope you don't mind me calling you Paul, and you must call me Rocco, as your daddy used to.'

'You knew my daddy?' Paul asked excitedly.

'Yes, he was a good friend of mine. When I was much younger he used to take me fishing and swimming, and we played all sorts of games together.'

'I have lots and lots of games, and when my daddy comes we play. You want to see, Rocco?' And trustingly Paul held out his hand to the man. 'They in the house.'

Rocco Andretti had said exactly the right thing to catch Paul's attention, Marlene thought rather sourly. Not only could he charm women, but children as well. Though she could not begrudge Paul the man's friendly advances. The boy had loved his father deeply, and missed him dreadfully. She had tried to explain, but Paul, at three, was a little too young to understand the finality of death. Recently he had been asking more and more if his daddy was coming back. It was a worry to Marlene, but she did not see what more she could do.

'You don't mind, do you, Ms Johanson?'

With a start Marlene looked up. Somehow Rocco Andretti was towering over her, and his eyes, lit with mocking triumph, caught and held hers.

She had been lost in her own thoughts. 'D-d-don't mind what?' she stuttered, struck anew by the overwhelming masculine appeal of the man standing only inches away from her. Luckily Paul came to her rescue.

'Roc can play with me, can't he, Mar?'

She looked down. Paul had already shortened the man's name to Roc, a habit of his, and was gazing up at her pleadingly, his small hand engulfed by the much larger · one of his new-found friend. She tried to discourage him. 'You have to have your tea now, Paul.'

'Please, after tea. He can stay for tea. Please, Mar.'

'I'm sure Mr Andretti can't stay that long, and Caterina...' She trailed off helplessly as it suddenly hit her that Caterina and Paul were brother and sister. She glanced up at the man in the forlorn hope that he would back her up. But no such luck...

'We have plenty of time,' he said flatly, leaving the ball firmly in her court.

Marlene looked back down at the grinning child and, smothering a sigh, said, 'Yes, of course.'

'Come on, Roc!' Paul cried in glee, and set off up the path as fast as his chubby legs would take him, the man in tow.

Caterina followed quickly, and it was left to Marlene to bring up the rear. She watched them disappear through the door in the wall and, following on, she turned and took a large bunch of keys from her pocket. She locked the door securely behind her and noted that the other three were almost at the entrance porch of the mellow old stone house she had called home almost all her life.

Inexplicably she shivered. She had a chilling premonition that unless she was very careful around Caterina Rossi and Rocco Andretti she might find herself in more trouble than she could handle, and possibly be shoved into the background of Paul's life for good. Over my dead body, she thought decisively.

'Hurry up, Mar. We're waiting!' Paul yelled.

Straightening her shoulders, she strolled across the gravel road to the house and, choosing another key from the bunch, unlocked the arched oak door and pushed it open.

'Welcome to our home,' she said politely, and if a trace of sarcasm echoed in the oak-panelled hall she didn't really care. She stood back and let the three of them walk past her. She took an apple from the bowl on the hall table and handed it to Paul. 'Take our friends through to the den and show them your toys. I'll give you a shout when tea is ready.' She badly needed some time alone to sort out her thoughts.

'Oh, no...!' Caterina began, obviously not wanting to play with Paul, but Rocco grabbed her arm and said something softly in his native language which Marlene did not catch, and they followed Paul along the hall to the back of the house.

With a sigh of relief Marlene took the first door on the left into the large farmhouse kitchen. She looked around at the familiar scrubbed pine furniture and the dried grasses and herbs hanging from the ceiling beams. She smiled and drew a deep, calming breath, then collapsed gratefully on the bentwood rocker set in front of the stone-mullioned window. She was just congratulating herself on getting rid of the Italian pair for a while when the door opened behind her.

She turned her head and once again was looking up into the harsh face of Rocco Andretti.

'I thought you were playing with Paul.'

'I told him I needed something from my car, but actually I want to speak to you in private.'

'Could it not wait until after we have tea?'

'No, there has been far too much delay in settling Paolo Rossi's affairs already. My own mother, who was a family friend of the Rossis, died only four months before him, and her estate is already wound up.'

'You have recently lost your mother?' Marlene asked softly, struck by the solemn tone of his deep voice.

'Yes, but to get back to the point,' Rocco said curtly, obviously not appreciating her sympathy, 'I think I can begin to understand why Paolo made the arrangements he did. In Italy the rule of law is closely connected to the church—an illegitimate child does not necessarily have the same rights as a child in England would. With you owning part of his company for so long he has obviously assured the financial independence of his son. That being the case, I'm sure I can persuade the family to come to a generous settlement over the shares and the property bequeathed in the will.'

He spoke as if he was doing her a favour, and she had to wonder why. Remembering the conversation she had overheard in the garden between Andretti and Caterina, Marlene tensed and rose to her feet. She looked into the dark, surprisingly compassionate face of Andretti, and wasn't fooled for a minute. Seduce her into compliance—get Paul and the villa that way? Fat Chance! she thought, and said bluntly, 'Young Paul was a much wanted and much loved son to his father, but he has absolutely nothing to do with you. And as for buying back the shares, I might not want to sell. They are mine... It is me you have to deal with.' She fixed him with her wide gold gaze. 'Me alone.'

They stared at each other, a tense silence stretching between them. Marlene refused to be the first to drop her gaze, and to her amazement Rocco suddenly smiled—a broad grin that took years off his age.

'You alone. I like that. But not here, not now. We cannot have a serious talk with the boy and Caterina around.'

'Rocco, where are you?' The demand, in Italian, echoed through the house, underlining his words.

'I think your lady-love has had enough of child-minding,' Marlene said cynically. 'If you will excuse me...' She made to walk past him, but he stepped in front of her. His long fingers caught her chin and tipped her face up to his.

'She is not my lady-love; I am reserving that position for you,' he declared outrageously.

Marlene's gasp of surprise was swallowed by hard, firm lips closing over her mouth and a darting tongue flicking the heated interior with stunning expertise. It was over so quickly she wondered if she had imagined it, but the racing of her pulse and the scarlet burn of her cheeks let her know it was all too real. 'You—you...' she spluttered.

'Get a baby-sitter for tomorrow night. I will pick you up at seven-thirty. You and I have a lot to discuss.'

She wanted to deny it, but at that moment Paul dashed into the kitchen with a furious-looking Caterina behind him, and the conversation became general.

The tea that followed was a disaster, the only one doing any talking being young Paul. Caterina was obviously bored to tears, and Marlene was still reeling from the effect of a single kiss. But at least after tea Rocco kept his word and played with Paul in the den for half an hour.

Later, when the guests were long gone and Marlene was tossing restlessly in her wide bed, she decided that that was the only good thing to have come out of the whole afternoon. She could console herself with the fact that Paul had for a short time thoroughly enjoyed himself with a man to play with—something that had been sadly lacking in his life of late.

Paul was not the only one lacking male companionship. She hadn't been out on a date with a man since she'd split with Julian the Toad, she thought wryly, and that had been over two years ago. In all honesty she had never felt deprived until today, when Rocco Andretti had appeared in her life.

Instant attraction! Instant lust! Whatever name she put on it, there was no denying that Rocco had had an amazing effect on her usually dormant libido. Just lying in bed thinking about him, and the kiss he had snatched, made her breasts swell and her nipples tighten in sensual need. Why now? And why him? she pondered. The one man in the world who seemed destined to be her enemy, and who obviously despised the sort of woman he thought she was.

Hot and restless, she turned over to lie on her back and stare at the ceiling, her mind spinning like a windmill. If it hadn't been for the promise she had given Paolo, she could have told Rocco Andretti the truth, at least about her career, but until she discovered who the traitor was in the late Paolo's firm she did not dare. A deep sigh escaped her. Wheels within wheels did not begin to describe her predicament.

Her mind went back to the first time she had met Paolo Rossi. She had left school the week before and had been awaiting the results of her exams to confirm her place at university—she had been accepted by the London School of Economics to read Economics and Languages. Her mother had gone into the village to deliver some feverfew plants—an old-fashioned but potent remedy for migraine—to Dr Branton, a man who was not afraid to mix the old with the new. Marlene had been in the house on her own when someone had rung the bell, and she had answered the door.

It was a man she had never seen before. Middle-aged—about fifty, she had thought. Tall, with steel-grey hair and dark brown eyes. He had stood looking at her in open-mouthed amazement.

'Yes? Can I help you?' she enquired.

'Marlene? Is it you?' he whispered, with the trace of an accent. Then he added, 'No, it can't be—you have to be nearly forty.'

'I am eighteen, thank you very much,' she replied cheekily. 'I think it must be my mum you want. We share the same name and everyone says I am very like her.' And that was the start of a great change in the lives of all three of them.

Her mother returned home and fainted at the sight of Paolo Rossi, and then it all came out. They had known each other years ago, when Paolo had been setting up the London branch of his company, and her mother had worked as a secretary in London. They had parted when Paolo had returned to his native Italy and married and had a daughter. Her mother had returned to Sussex and married her cousin, the then manager of the market garden, and had given birth to the younger Marlene Johanson.

His reason for looking up her mother after so long was simple. He had recently had a minor heart attack and, heeding the warning, had taken a long, hard look at his life and hadn't liked what he saw. So he had decided to take time out from his hectic work schedule to look up his old friends, to 'smell the roses', before it was too late. Paolo now lived in his London apartment almost permanently, only visiting his native Italy when business demanded it.

He and Marlene's mother became lovers. At first Marlene was angry, and a bit wary of the new man in her mother's life. With the idealism of youth she thought it was wrong, but she could not deny that he made her mother very happy. And, according to Paolo, his marriage had been a sham for years. The Contessa had married him for his money and he had married her because she was pregnant—nothing else. She considered him to be beneath her in every way, an ill-bred self-made man.

Finally, when young Paul was born, and although he was Catholic, he asked his wife for a divorce. The Contessa refused and went on refusing right up to Paolo's death.

Over the years he spent a lot of time at the Johanson house in the country, and was instrumental in helping Marlene through university and getting her her first job with a city stockbroker. He was like a second father to her—more, because she could barely remember her own father. Paolo was there for Marlene when her one and only romance with the rat Julian broke up, and again when her mother died.

When Paolo asked for her help in bringing up young Paul she willingly gave up her job in the City and returned to the country to look after her little brother. But the death of her mother had had a disastrous effect on Paolo, and he never really recovered.

By the time he realised someone was working against him in Italy, trying to take control of his business, it was too late for him to do much about it. He was too ill. Hence the promise he elicited from Marlene to discover what was going on and try to prevent the destruction of his good name... Of course Marlene vowed to help all she could, but secretly she thought when he died that it wasn't so much a heart attack as a broken heart that had killed him.

Marlene yawned widely now and turned onto her side, pulling the sheet up around her neck. Reliving the past did no good, she thought sleepily. Tomorrow was for the living. And she had finally reached a decision on the other promise Paulo had extracted from her—to take his son to Italy for two months every year and let him get to know the land of his father's birth.

He had even gone so far as to leave young Paul the family villa in Amalfi in his will, according to the letter from the London firm of solicitors which had been lying on her dressing table for months. It still hurt her a little that Paolo had thought it necessary to make his request for his son to visit Italy official, as though he had not quite trusted her completely to carry out his wishes. But then again, she couldn't blame him. His view on the female sex's ability to be truthful had always been somewhat biased by the actions of his Italian wife and, in a way, of her own mother, she supposed.

School was due to finish this Friday, the twenty-sixth of July, for eight weeks. She could procrastinate no longer. The decision had really been taken for her, with the arrival of Rocco Andretti and Caterina. Even before that, really. With the arrival of the solicitor's letter, if she was honest. Tomorrow she would make the arrangements for Paul and herself to fly to Italy at the weekend. As for Rocco Andretti, she would have dinner with him tomorrow night, listen to his offer for her shares and, with Caterina's words in the forefront of her mind, beware of any attempt he might make to try and seduce her into parting with either them or Paul.

She had made it her business to know that an extraordinary general meeting of Rossi International had been called for Friday the second of August, to discuss the disappointing performance of the company and appoint a new MD. Marlene had been considering keeping a low profile and dealing with the problem through the London lawyers, but after meeting Caterina and Andretti, and after having been roundly insulted by both, she now determined to discover exactly what was going on and hopefully reveal the truth at the board meeting in August in person.

In fact, she quite relished the challenge. Andretti could not be that sharp, despite appearances, because he could quite simply have checked that the Ms M. Johanson on the present share certificate was not the same Mrs M. Johanson who had owned them earlier.

She loved her young brother, and did not regret living in the country for the past two years for his benefit. She found the occasional stint in the garden quite therapeutic, though her main interest was still finance—she did miss the cut and thrust of the dealing floor sometimes . . .

Another wide yawn, and minutes later she was asleep.

Marlene stretched her hands above her head in an attempt to get the crick out of her back and took one last look at the computer screen before switching it off. She had instituted a few lines of enquiry with friends in the City and on the international markets. Very soon she should have the information she sought.

If Andretti could see her now, she thought with a smile, he would get one hell of a shock. As she swivelled around in her chair, her glance skimmed the banks of machinery installed in the attic room she used as her office. She had not given up her career on the death of her mother. With all the high technology now available she simply worked from home as a consultant for numerous finance houses.

Pushing back her chair, she stood up and walked out of the room, locking the door behind her and quickly descending the narrow staircase to the first floor and her bedroom. Paul was all right. Jean had taken him to stay at her house for the night and she had the house to herself.

Stripping off her shirt and shorts, she crossed to the wardrobes that filled one wall and slid back a mirrored door. Her mouth twisted in a regretful grimace as she surveyed the Calvin Klein and Donna Karan suits, separates and dresses—her favourite designers and her usual choice. Sliding back another door, she rummaged at the very end of the rail and finally found what she was looking for. A cotton frock she had not worn in years. Yes! Just the image she wanted to portray. Caterina and Andretti thought she was some kind of ignorant, immoral peasant. Who was she to disillusion them? She asked herself, a secret smile curling her wide mouth as she walked into the small but luxurious *ensuite* shower room.

Half an hour later, with her blonde hair washed and dried and left loose to flow in waves down her back almost to her waist, and with the minimum of make-up, she surveyed herself in the mirror and almost laughed out loud.

Physically she had been a late developer, and at eighteen she had been a lot smaller in the bust department. Now the autumnal-coloured Indian cotton dress barely caught her shoulders and strained across the full curves of her high breasts. The bodice buttoned down the front and cinched in at her waist, then swirled out over her hips to reach to mid-calf. Green espadrilles were tied around her ankles and she looked like a hippie from the sixties. Absolutely right for the part she was about to play, she told herself, and, with a casual flick at an errant strand of hair floating over her breast, she left the bedroom and went downstairs.

Marlene had barely reached the hall when the doorbell rang, not once but three times. Sharp and impatient, she thought, and was in no doubt as to who her caller was. Taking a deep, calming breath, she opened the door.

Her breath stopped in her chest and her eyes widened in helpless awe at the picture Rocco Andretti presented. Gone was the casually dressed man of yesterday afternoon, and in his place was a hard, sophisticated businessman. It showed in the dark blue three-piece suit, immaculately tailored to fit his large frame. The brilliant white shirt contrasted sharply with his bronzed features, and the Paisley silk tie in muted blues added just the right conservative touch. She could easily picture him in a court of law, dominant and dynamic.

Unconsciously she took a step backwards, her eyes lifting to the strong face, and she was caught in the hard glitter of his dark gaze. It would take a brave person to try and go against this man, was her immediate thought. Or a fool. Unable to tear her eyes away, she had the sinking sensation that she was the fool...

'Are you going to ask me in? Or stand here all night admiring the view?' he demanded, his predatory gaze roving over her body with undisguised sexual insolence.

'What? Yes—no. I'm ready,' she blustered and, taking a step forward, pulled the door closed behind her.

'Such punctuality in a woman. I am impressed,' Rocco declared, cupping her elbow with one large hand and staring down into her blushing face.

His smile was incredible—a flash of brilliant white teeth, eyes that gleamed with pleasure and something more... a blatant appreciation that set her pulse racing. He led her to a long, low-slung sports car and opened the door, watching her manoeuvre herself into the bucket seat and grinning broadly as her dress hitched up, revealing a length of bare, shapely leg. Then, closing the door, he swung around the front to the driver's seat and slid in beside her.

Marlene was speechless. For some reason he had the ability to make her behave like a love-sick teenager, and she did not like it. He angered her and attracted her both at the same time, and she seemed unable to do anything about it. The engine roared to life, the car shot down the long drive and out onto the road, and she still had not got her breath back.

'A quiet woman, as well as beautiful. Quite a combination,' Rocco said, flashing her a sidelong glance. 'They say the best courtesans in history all shared the same ability to be good listeners.' He smiled sardonically, his gaze dropping for a second to the soft curve of her breasts revealed by the scoop neck of her dress, before returning to the road ahead. 'Along with other, more earthy attributes, of course,' he added. 'Which I am sure you also have in abundance.'

If he had not been driving Marlene would have hit him for his scandalous remark, but at least it had the effect of bringing her out of her stupid fascination with the physical perfection of the man and back to reality. 'My attributes or lack of them are none of your affair,' she said curtly. 'This is supposed to be a business meeting and I will thank you to keep it that way.'

'For a country girl who has spent most of her adult life as an old man's mistress, your indignation seems a touch out of place, Marlene.'

'Ms Johanson to you,' she shot back. Hearing her name on his tongue seemed oddly intimate, and she needed all her wits about her for the next few hours.

'If you think I am going to call you Ms Johanson all night, forget it, Marlene. Given your occupation over the past few years, calling yourself Ms seems a bit of a cheek. As I understand it, that particular form of address is used for hard-hitting businesswomen—hardly suitable for an old man's mistress.'

'All right, Miss Johanson will be perfectly acceptable,' she conceded.

'Marlene, there is something you should know about me. I like my women malleable and I insist you call me Rocco. There is no way I am spending the next couple of months arguing with you over a name. Understood?'

'Two months?' she exclaimed in astonishment, the colour draining from her face. He could not possibly know she had decided to go to Italy. She had only decided herself last night. Was the man a mind-reader or what? 'You're staying in England that long?' she queried.

'I have a couple of months' vacation, and if you make it worth my while I rather think I might,' he drawled throatily. 'What do you say, Marlene? You and me together.'

'Worth your while?' she snapped back, ignoring the breathless feeling the idea of spending time with Rocco gave her. 'I don't pay for men; I prefer it the other way round,' she said tartly. Then it hit her. Of course, Rocco knew the terms of the will and didn't want her to go to Italy. He was quite prepared to spend weeks in England playing the besotted lover if it stopped Marlene claiming young Paul's inheritance.

His deep shout of laughter broke into her muddled thoughts. 'I am beginning to see why Rossi was so enamoured of you, Marlene. You are quite a challenge.' And before she could ask him what he meant the car had stopped outside an imposing country house and Rocco was sliding out of the driver's seat.

Her door was opened with a flourish. 'Harlton Grange. I am informed it is a good place to eat. Shall we go?'

Marlene knew the Grange, and for a second she regretted her ancient summer dress. And then a bigger worry hit her.

'Yes.' She reluctantly murmured her assent and, stepping out of the car, meekly allowed Rocco to take her arm and usher her up the wide stone steps to the entrance hall. She had been here before—quite a few times, in fact—but never dressed like a charity shop reject!

Harlton Grange was the best restaurant in the county, and was often used by members of the business establishment not only locally but from the City as well. Besides that, The Johanson Herb Garden provided the restaurant with its products. She knew most of the staff, and it was quite possible that someone who knew her real career might inadvertently make a comment about it and blow her cover.

The prospect of keeping Rocco Andretti in the dark about her relationship with Paolo Rossi and young Paul, never mind her actual field of expertise, was looking remoter by the second. She could have kicked herself for not asking where he was taking her to dine. If she had not been so bowled over by the man's pure animal magnetism she might have done so. But it was too late now and, stifling a sigh, she casually flicked a swath of her long hair, seemingly artlessly, so that it fell down over her shoulder, hiding one side of her face.

As a disguise it failed dismally. A voice boomed out, 'Good evening, Miss Johanson. This is a pleasure.' Deep blue eyes set in a handsome face looked her over in puzzlement. Henry, the head waiter, could have been a double for Paul Newman, and she smiled back at him, knowing his surprise was at the state of her dress, though he was far too much of a gentleman to comment.

'Business doing well? Still rolling it in?' he asked with a grin.

'Oh, yes, yes.' She rushed to respond before Henry could put his foot in it completely and ask her for a tip on what shares to invest his money in—something he was prone to do every time he saw her. 'The Herb Garden is doing brilliantly. I hope the chef is still happy with the produce?'

'Yes, of course—best in the country, as ever. But—'

Luckily for Marlene, before Henry could go on Rocco cut in. 'I have a booking. Rocco Andretti,' he said curtly, his brows drawing together in an unsmiling look at the other man. 'And the lady is my guest.'

Henry glanced up at Rocco and straightened perceptibly, once more the immaculate *maître d'*. 'Yes, of course, sir. A table for two. This way, please.'

Marlene almost grinned. Poor Henry had been instantly quelled by the air of authority Rocco displayed. But one glance at Rocco's forbidding countenance and all thought of amusement left her.

Long fingers tightened perceptibly around her bare arm. 'You appear to be well known here, Marlene. Rossi brought you here, did he?'

'On occasions,' she said coolly as she was ushered through the large, ornately carved arched doors into the dining room. She glanced around quickly and sighed with relief. It was a Tuesday night and there were not many diners—and none she knew, thank God! With an upsurge of confidence, she continued casually, 'But we also supply the Grange with fresh herbs—they are old and valued customers. Henry and I are good friends.'

'It seems to me any man over fifty is your *good friend*. What is it? Looking for a father figure, are you? Or simply frightened a younger man might demand more than your sort can give?'

'You know absolutely nothing about my "sort", Mr Andretti, and if you intend to spend the evening insulting me we might as well leave now,' Marlene snapped back, and, freeing her arm from his hold, she would have walked out.

But Rocco grabbed her wrist and halted her in midstride. Bending his dark head towards her, he husked, 'Forgive me,' and brushed her brow with warm lips. 'I find I have difficulty accepting the thought of you in bed with Rossi. And watching the even older Henry ogle you does nothing for my temper.'

His apology and light kiss were so unexpected, and the implication of jealousy so surprising, that Marlene stared blankly up at him.

Urging her towards the table, Rocco said, 'Please sit down,' and, pulling out a chair before the waiter could reach it, he hovered over her until she obeyed.

Her skin still warm from the heat of his mouth, she nervously straightened the cutlery on the table, at the same time watching with wary eyes as Rocco took the chair opposite. Without realising what was happening she found one of her hands covered by his.

'Pax for the rest of the evening, hmm?' he drawled softly.

His large hand engulfing hers sent shivers up her spine, and the seemingly casual way his thumb rubbed her palm made her flesh tingle. Hastily pulling her hand free, she mumbled, 'All right,' and gratefully took the menu the waiter was holding out to her.

Pax? A feeling of peace was the last thing Rocco Andretti aroused in her! Quite the reverse, in fact. He had an uncanny ability to make her pulse go into overdrive and her knees go weak. Not a good way to feel about a man she was trying to deceive, she thought wryly, with a growing conviction that it was going to be a very fraught evening.

CHAPTER THREE

MARLENE held the menu in front of her face, apparently studying it, but in reality she didn't read a word; she simply needed a moment to recover her self-control.

'Typical female—can't make up her mind,' Rocco commented in a flippant aside to the hovering waiter as his hand once more covered Marlene's and lowered her menu down to the table. 'Allow me to order for you.'

'Typical male chauvinist,' she responded coolly, quickly withdrawing her hand. And, ignoring the gleam in her companion's dark eyes, she tilted her head back and bestowed a brilliant smile on the waiter. 'I'll have the melon with the almond trout to follow.'

'An excellent choice, and just to show you I am not the male chauvinist you imagine I will have the same,' Rocco responded, and, leaning back in his chair, his body at ease, he stunned her with a slow, dangerously sexy smile.

She blushed and looked away, glancing around the room—anywhere rather than at the man opposite, who seemed to radiate a lethal charm without even trying. She noticed the covetous glances cast in his direction by the other females present and knew exactly how they felt. No one man had the right to look so good, and if she felt a tinge of triumph because he was with her who could blame her? she thought smugly as, in her peripheral vision, she registered the arrival of the wine waiter and Rocco's casual order of a bottle of the best champagne.

'Until I know a woman's taste intimately, I find champagne is usually acceptable,' he opined, his dark eyes seeking hers. 'Don't you agree, Marlene?'

Ignoring the innuendo, she said, 'I'm not much of a drinker, but I'm sure you're right.'

'I am right about most things,' Rocco drawled. 'Bear that in mind when we get down to business later.'

'Why later?' she asked bluntly.

'Because I have no intention of spoiling a fine meal with business, so relax and enjoy,' he commanded as the waiter deftly uncorked the bottle with a reassuring pop and filled two glasses with the sparkling liquid.

Grasping her glass, Marlene raised it to her lips and took a hasty swallow. She needed it to shore up her dwindling confidence where Rocco was concerned. Was it just her, or could he possibly be feeling the same fierce physical attraction as she did? she puzzled, before responding, 'I am relaxed.' Then, meeting his dark gaze with slightly more self-confidence, she added, 'And I am quite capable of discussing business and eating at the same time.'

'I am sure you are capable of many interesting things.' A teasing smile curved his hard mouth. 'I hope to discover that for myself eventually.' He glanced down to where her full breasts strained against the fabric of her dress, making her tremble with awareness. He noted her reaction, his glittering eyes clashing with hers, and, raising his glass, he said, 'A toast to business and our closer association. May there be a successful conclusion to both.' He took a sip of the champagne before adding, 'But for now let us concentrate on eating . . . Other appetites can wait.'

If he did not stop this sexual innuendo she was liable to clock him one, but, perhaps luckily for Rocco, at that moment the first course arrived.

Surprisingly the meal passed with remarkable ease. When he set out to charm Rocco had no equal. They

discussed neutral topics—the theatre, music, the opera—
and he regaled her with stories of his travels in far-flung
corners of the world that had Marlene laughing out loud.
It did cross her mind that for a lawyer he did an awful
lot of travelling, but she dismissed the thought.

They had finished their meal and the bottle of champagne and were sipping their coffee when the warning
bells rang loud in Marlene's head. A head definitely hazy
with champagne.

'Tell me,' Rocco demanded suddenly, 'how old are
you?'

'Twenty-six... But don't you know it's an insult to
ask a lady her age?' she quipped with a grin.

'Some lady!' His mouth twisted cynically. 'That makes
you only eighteen when you took Rossi, a married man,
as your lover.'

She looked up sharply, her golden eyes glinting with
anger, and almost blurted out the truth—that Paolo had
been her late mother's lover. But common sense prevailed. Perhaps the coffee had had a sobering effect as
it hit her. Rocco had drunk very little champagne, she
realised. She had quaffed the lion's share. Straightening
in her seat, she responded with contrived flippancy.
'Eighteen is over the age of consent.'

'So young to be so mercenary,' he taunted savagely.
'Perhaps it is time we got down to business after all.'

'I could not agree more. Fire away.' She flashed him
an insolent smile. 'But keep it simple. Remember I am
a country girl, with a very tenuous grasp of financial
matters.' She was lying through her teeth, but his callous
comment on her character had stiffened her resolve. Plus
the fact that she did not trust him an inch...

His hooded lids lowered over his black eyes, masking
his expression, and his deep voice softened considerably.
'Yes, I suppose you are, and as such I should not judge
you too harshly. It takes two to start an affair, and Rossi,
at his age, should have had more sense than to seduce

an innocent eighteen-year-old girl. You *were* innocent when you met him, I take it?'

He did not deserve an answer, but, in keeping with the character she was trying to portray, she decided to give him one. 'Certainly,' she shot back truthfully. 'I have only ever had one lover.' Again, it was the truth. The fact that the one lover had not been Paolo Rossi was her secret. 'And I really miss Paolo—he was so good to me. Which is why I must try to do what Paolo would have wanted with my shares in the company. It is a worry. The market garden is quite simple to run, but big business I don't understand too well.' Silently she hoped she had not laid it on too thick.

'I understand your feelings, Marlene, and you have nothing to worry about, I promise,' Rocco said, and to a casual observer his expression would have appeared to be one of sincere concern. 'I am here to help you.'

But Marlene was not fooled for a second. She wanted to laugh at the change in his manner, so obviously false! It was only by taking a sip of coffee that she managed to hide her grin. Pull the other one! she thought, but said nothing.

'I want to do what is best for you and your child,' Rocco assured her.

If she had not known better Marlene would have sworn the sincerity in his tone was genuine, and when his eyes met hers the compassion in his gaze had her marvelling at his acting ability. 'Thank you for that,' she gushed, no slouch in the acting department herself.

'I know it must be hard for you, losing your lover and being left with complex financial arrangements to deal with, but I intend to make it very simple.'

'Please do,' she encouraged huskily, gazing limply at his rugged face.

'As you know, Rossi put twenty-four per cent of his company shares in your name a few years ago. He voted them himself, of course, but since his death the London office has, quite naturally, as you are the official owner of the shares, sent information on the company to you. Whether you read it or not, or understood it, I don't know.' One dark brow arched quizzically, and Marlene did not disappoint him.

'I glanced at a few letters, but I can't say I understood too well,' she said, and once again she had to bite her lip to stop the grin threatening to break out when she recognised the gleam of triumph in his eyes.

'To put it simply, Rossi International is in a bit of a slump, and at the present time the share price is low. One pound fifty at close of business today. Also, the majority stockholders have called an extraordinary board meeting at the beginning of August to try and rectify the situation. Unfortunately until then, and until some salvage package is arranged, the price is liable to drop a lot lower.

'Now, I know you won't want to get involved in the technicalities. Your main interest must be to obtain the best price and assure your son's financially secure future. That is why I am here at the Contessa's request. Both she and her daughter realise Paolo must have been very fond of the boy, but he must also have known there was no way a young woman like you would want to get involved in what is basically still an Italian company. Worrying about finance and board meetings is not your style. They are quite willing to buy the shares back, and have authorised me to offer you...' Rocco paused, allowing a small smile to curve his mouth.

Now we come to the nitty-gritty, Marlene thought drily. 'Offer me what?' she asked eagerly. She was silently thinking that the true market value of the company, as perceived by the leading market gurus, was more like four pounds a share. It was only the machinations in Italy that had brought the price so low.

'They are prepared to be quite generous, because they understand your position as an unmarried mother, and of course they want to make sure the company stays in the family as a tribute to Rossi's achievements. Therefore they will happily pay you two pounds a share.' Rocco leant back in his seat, confidence oozing from every pore. 'It is a brilliant offer, and you can be sure no one is trying to cheat you.'

Marlene watched as his hand slid into the breast pocket of his jacket and he withdrew a business card.

'This is a leading firm of stockbrokers in the City. Ring them tomorrow and check for yourself. They will confirm that the price I have quoted is the truth and that the Contessa's offer is truly generous, I assure you.' And then he mentioned the total amount in pounds sterling.

'So much!' she exclaimed, as he obviously expected, and responded to the self-satisfied if derisory smile he bestowed upon her with equal mock innocence.

'It will certainly keep you and your boy in the manner to which you are accustomed.'

This man could sell ice to eskimos, Marlene thought, her eyes roaming over his darkly attractive face. His oh, so concerned expression! Reaching out her hand, she took the card. Her fingers touched his, and a disturbing flash of awareness made her draw back quickly and glance down at the card in her hand to hide the sudden flush of colour to her cheeks. She recognised the name of the firm even as she battled with the unwanted emotions his slightest touch aroused.

'I'm sure you're right, and I will ring these people.' She waved the card in front of her face, which was red with a mixture of anger and arousal. 'First thing in the morning.'

'There is no great hurry for your answer,' Rocco drawled complacently, his chiselled mouth curving in a confident grin. 'How about I call for you at seven-thirty again on Thursday? We can repeat this delightful meal over again, and you can give me your answer then.'

Once more he reached across the table and caught her hands in his, and, turning them both palm up, he added, 'As for the Will—the property in Italy—I'm sure the Contessa will come to some equitable agreement over that as well. You really have nothing to worry about.' And, bending his head, he lifted her cupped hands and pressed a kiss in each palm. Marlene felt the effect of his kisses right down to her toes, and could not have pulled her hands free even if she had wanted to. But at that precise moment she had no such inclination. Instead, she looked down at his bent head and had an overwhelming urge to run her fingers through his thick black hair. She shivered, and Rocco looked up at her through long black lashes, his dark eyes gleaming with sensuality.

'Rossi was a very lucky man, but he is dead. It is time you cut all ties with the past and moved on. I want you...' he drawled throatily.

She caught her breath, and in that second wanted Rocco more than any man she had ever met. Until he spoke again.

'I want you to let me help you do that.' He sat back, freeing her hands. 'Believe me, you and Paul need not visit Italy or meet the Contessa. I will arrange everything.'

Marlene had not blushed in years, but around this man she seemed to be doing it all the time, she thought with rising fury, knowing that he had deliberately played on her attraction to him, hesitating over his 'I want you' simply to tease her.

She looked across at him and her mouth tightened in a grim line. He looked like the cat that had swallowed the canary. In fact, she would not have been surprised if he had licked his lips, so confident was he that he had her exactly where he wanted her. It would have been funny except that she found little amusement in knowing that the only man she had been attracted to in years was trying to cheat her.

Obviously he thought that seducing her into staying in England and so forfeiting the property by the terms of the Will would be a whole lot easier than trying the same thing in Italy and then having to prove her an unfit mother. He was a devious swine. No mistake. But she had been deceived by a man before and had vowed never again. The self-knowledge gave her the courage to continue with her plan.

Wide-eyed, and forcing her expression into one of suitable awe, she simpered, 'It is kind of you to offer to help me. But I hardly know you. I really could not put you to so much trouble. I will check with this firm tomorrow, as you said—' she carefully placed the card in her purse '—but I don't think I should rush into anything.' And she meant it both ways. Business and pleasure.

Deliberately folding her arms beneath her bust, she rested on the table and leant towards Rocco, revealing an even greater amount of cleavage than her too small dress already allowed. She saw his eyes drop down and the gleam of lust in their darkening depths, and she hid a little smile before dropping her bombshell.

'You see, Rocco, Paolo asked me to take his son to Italy, to give the boy a taste of his father's birthplace, and he reaffirmed his request in his Will. I could not possibly defy the wishes of a dead man, so I have booked our seats and Paul and I fly out on Saturday. As I am going to be in Italy when the board meeting takes place I might as well go. And after that I might consider selling my shares, but not before.'

The confusion in his expression was a joy to behold. He did not know where to look—the ripe curve of her breast or her beautiful, seemingly innocent face. His lips compressed and temper flared briefly in his black eyes, then his gaze narrowed assessingly on her lovely face.

'Let me get this straight. Your flight is booked, you are leaving at the weekend and you intend turning up at the board meeting?'

'Yes.' Marlene sat back and, tilting her head to one side, added, 'It will be quite an adventure—a holiday in a foreign country. Paul and I are really looking forward to it.'

'But you don't even speak the language,' he grated, his exasperation showing.

'I've bought a phrase book,' Marlene shot back airily. 'We'll manage just fine. I believe Amalfi is lovely at this time of year.'

'You have been busy since yesterday.' His eyes narrowed acutely on her face, as if he was trying to read what was behind her bland smile. Then, abruptly pushing his chair back, he stood up. 'Let's get out of here,' he said, and, signalling to the waiter for the bill, glanced back down at Marlene.

'I am beginning to think there is more to you than meets the eye.' His gaze lingered on the soft swell of her firm breasts and rather daring cleavage. 'And god knows what *is* on show would tempt the Pope himself,' he declared, pure male frustration lacing his voice.

Marlene hid a grin as she meekly got to her feet. Smoothing down the skirt of her dress over her slim hips, she said, 'I thought you would be pleased, Rocco. You did imply you wanted to get to know me better,' she could not resist taunting.

He slanted her a black, flaring glance before dropping a handful of notes on the table, and then, taking her arm, urged her towards the door. 'So I did,' he murmured, almost to himself, as they walked out of the dining room. 'But I rather hoped to keep it discreet. And somehow, with you in Italy...' He shook his dark head and, turning, caught her by the shoulders and looked into her eyes. 'Are you sure you want to meet Rossi's legitimate family? Expose young Paul to what might be a negative experience? They have to suffer you as a shareholder, but they don't have to like it. Be sensible— let me arrange a deal with the Contessa for the villa, for everything.'

Marlene could feel the warmth of his hands on her shoulders, and the subtle male scent of him filled her nostrils. She felt dizzy, staring up into his tanned, attractive face, and for a second she wanted to agree to whatever he said. He looked so genuinely concerned for her and her young brother. A rush of cool air as someone entered the restaurant brought her back to her senses. 'No, it's all arranged,' she said, and, shrugging off his hands, she headed for the exit.

Sitting in the passenger seat of the car, she cast a sidelong glance at Rocco as he guided the vehicle expertly through the twisting back roads towards her home. His hawk-like profile, his long fingers curled loosely but in complete control around the steering wheel, the movement of the muscles in his thighs so close to her own as he shifted through the gears all had an unsettling effect on her brain, already overheated with champagne. She found herself imagining what his handsome features would look like taut with passion, what his hands would feel like controlling her... And then an uneasy thought struck her. He was a dynamic, powerful man and yet he had given up far too easily, with hardly a murmur...

Sensing her scrutiny, Rocco sent her a brief glance, one dark brow arched quizzically. She shook her head and, swallowing hard, looked away. He was remarkably quiet, and she could feel the sexual tension building between them with every mile they travelled. But perhaps it was just her over-fertile imagination, she told herself sternly, and made herself look out of the side window until they arrived at her home.

'Are you going to ask me in for coffee?' Rocco demanded as he held out a hand to help her out of the car.

Marlene put her hand in his and stood up. 'No' trembled on her tongue as her fingers curved around his, delighting in the sudden warmth of his grasp, but the sound that came out of her mouth was, 'Yes.' Hastily she pulled her hand free and darted for the door.

Her fingers fumbled with the big old key and Rocco's hand closed over hers again. He took the key from her unresisting fingers and opened the door. She stepped over the threshold with Rocco at her side. She had left a lamp lit on the hall table, and somehow the panelled hall suddenly seemed very intimate. She dropped her bag on the table as Rocco closed the door behind them.

'Welcoming,' Rocco murmured and, swinging her round to face him with a hand on her shoulder, he tilted her chin with his index finger. 'I wonder if the hostess is as welcoming?' His voice was a husky purr.

Marlene watched immobile, a prisoner of her own desire, as his dark head bent lower and his firm mouth settled softly over hers. The kiss was like no other she had experienced. His lips swept light as a butterfly wing, then withdrew, only to return and nibble at her full bottom lip. His tongue traced the outline of her mouth and her lips parted on a sigh as she leant into the hard warmth of his large body, her eyes closing as his tongue sought the inner secrets of her mouth.

She felt heat pool low in her stomach, and she knew she had been waiting for this all evening, however much she tried to deny it. She wanted his kiss, his taste and a whole lot more—everything he had to offer, she finally admitted, and surrendered to the pleasure he promised.

Her tongue started a voyage of discovery of its own. She loved the warmth of his mouth and, lifting a slender hand, she cupped one side of his face, the slightly rough texture a tactile delight. She loved kissing him. His hard, firm lips were like no other man's in the universe, she was convinced. She delighted in the pressure of his hands on her shoulders, the way he deepened the kiss, probing

and possessive. Her other arm snaked up around his neck
and she threaded her fingers through the silky black hair
of his head, something else she had been wanting to do
all evening.

He lifted his mouth from hers, finally allowing her to
catch her breath. His large hands slid from her
shoulders—one to her waist, the other to cup her
bottom—holding her hard against him, making her
aware of his bulging masculine arousal. She looked up
through her lashes into his brilliant black eyes, her heart
racing, her lips swollen from his kisses, her mind blank.

'I knew it would be like this,' Rocco drawled huskily,
and with a brief, fierce hug he eased her away from him.
'But not yet, my sexy siren.'

Marlene was not sure she liked 'sexy siren'. A moment
later she knew she did not as slowly she regained her
senses. She could not help being aware that Rocco, with
a brief, bland smile at her flushed face, had recovered
from their passionate interlude remarkably quickly, while
she was still shaken and totally mortified by her spineless
surrender.

'This time business first,' he said, and, brushing past
her, he opened the door into the kitchen. 'You make the
coffee and then we will put all our cards on the table.'

Following him into her own kitchen, Marlene battled
to recover her former poise. If looks could have killed
he would have had a dagger in his back.

'Agreed, Marlene?' he prompted.

'I don't know what you mean.' Was he suspicious?
'All our cards on the table' sounded ominous, but still
she added coolly, 'I already have.' And, crossing the
kitchen floor on none too steady legs, she set about
making the coffee—without looking at Rocco.

'I think not.'

Ignoring his comment, she took two cups from the
cupboard above her head and the milk from the refrigerator; the sugar bowl was standing on the bench.

'Amazing—so much activity for a cup of coffee.' Rocco's cynically voiced comment scraped over her frayed nerves. 'One could almost believe you were nervous. Now, why is that, I wonder? You're hardly the shrinking violet type, afraid to be alone with a man.'

Slowly she turned around and leant against the bench for support. He was sitting with legs astride one of the pine chairs, his arms folded on the high back, propping up his dark head, looking incredibly sexy with his black hair ruffled from her earlier ministrations. 'You said you wanted coffee, and that is all you are getting,' she snapped, resenting the way he had made her feel with a simple kiss. Well, not so simple! she admitted in her mind. But seeing him sitting there so at ease when her insides were still churning was infuriating.

'What are you so afraid of, Marlene?' he asked silkily. 'Surely not of me? I'm simply your basic man, and we both know your experience in that department.'

'Nothing—I'm not afraid of anything at all.' Turning back to the percolator, she quickly filled two cups with the steaming brew. Basic in his desires, certainly, but there was nothing in the least simple about Rocco Andretti, she reminded herself forcibly, before asking, 'Black or white?'

'Black, no sugar—and come and sit down. You're hovering there like a humming-bird poised for flight.'

Marlene stirred sugar and milk into her own cup with obsessive determination, until finally she could delay no longer without melting the spoon! Taking a deep breath, she picked up both cups and turned around. She carefully placed a cup in front of Rocco on the scrubbed table, before crossing to the opposite side of the table and sitting down. She cradled her cup in her hands and looked at him over the top of it. He lifted his to his mouth and drained it in one go.

'Now that's out of the way. Not bad coffee for an Englishwoman, actually,' he murmured, and swinging back round on the chair, he leant his elbows on the table and fixed her with dark, intent eyes. 'I am going to be honest with you, Marlene.'

That will be a first! She took a deep swallow of her coffee, thinking for a horrible moment that she had spoken out loud. But Rocco was still speaking, so obviously she had not. Thank God! She needed all her wits about her to deal with him... No easy task, when a simple look from his deep brown eyes had the power to make her skin burn.

'The offer I made on behalf of the Contessa for the shares was perfectly fair, as you will find out when you check tomorrow. But as for the villa, and the conditions set out in Rossi's will, it must be obvious to you the whole idea is ridiculous.'

'Ridiculous?' She tilted her head to one side, studying him curiously. 'Why ridiculous? It seems perfectly straightforward to me, but no doubt you, with your superior intellect, know better,' she drawled sarcastically.

He had to be the most casual lawyer she had ever met. His firm had drawn up the will; if it was so ridiculous he should have advised his client at the time, not come here after the man was dead and try to negate it. But then maybe Italian lawyers were like that! What did she know? As a student she had visited Italy twice, once to Florence and once to Venice, and she had spent most of her time in the art galleries. She knew next to nothing about Italian law.

'We both know your sudden desire to fulfil Rossi's wish for your son to spend two months at the villa in Amalfi every year for the next five years is simply so you can claim the property for Paul. True, it is the condition laid down in the will. But even you cannot be that mercenary.'

'Maybe I am,' she said, stung by his insult. Actually, she had no idea how much the villa was worth and cared even less. She was going to Italy to fulfil her own promise to Paolo Rossi. She had more than enough money of her own, but Rocco didn't know that...

'What kind of mother are you?' His tone was biting, cynical. 'Have you thought of the harm it might do the boy? The unpleasantness that will ensue? The Contessa will make sure everyone knows the boy is a bastard and the family will certainly not recognise him, even while they make sure you adhere to the absolute letter of the will.'

'She would do that?' Marlene exclaimed in disgust.

'And worse,' Rocco said flatly. 'Southern Italy is nothing like England. Unmarried mothers are still frowned on. The Contessa is a leader in society; she can make it very difficult for you and the boy, if not downright impossible. You seem to love the boy, but two months can seem a very long time with only a child to talk to. Surely you can see it would be much easier for everyone involved if you took the Contessa's offer for your shares, and I'm sure I can persuade her to reach monetary solution—compensation—in the question of the villa as well. You need never set foot in Italy.'

Stunned by his duplicity, Marlene drained her coffee-cup and replaced it on the table, not daring to look at him. It saddened her to think that the man sitting opposite her, the man she was undeniably seriously attracted to, was so lacking in any sense of loyalty. He was Rossi's lawyer, and by his own admission a friend. Yet he cared nothing for his late client's wishes and would quite happily betray them to please the Contessa. Even going so far as to try and buy Marlene's shares in the company for half of what they were worth. It was despicable behaviour, and if it wasn't illegal it ought to be...

'Well, have we a basis for a deal?' Rocco's deep voice broke the lengthening silence.

Marlene shook her head in disbelief. She was beginning to see why Paolo had spent most of his time in England, as far away from his estranged wife as he could get. The woman was obviously a first-class manipulator. She had to be to have persuaded a man like Rocco Andretti to go against his lawyer's training and do her bidding.

'Was that shake of your head a no?' Rocco demanded sharply.

'I haven't decided yet.' Her lips twisted in a cynical smile. 'I need to know more about the family first. Tell me...' She pinned him with a gimlet gaze. 'The aristocracy has been defunct in Italy for years. Why did Signora Rossi insist on retaining her title of Contessa?' And, disgusted by the whole sordid mess, Marlene shoved back her chair and got to her feet, not bothering to hide her anger. 'Descendant of Lucretia Borgia, was she? She certainly sounds like it.'

Rocco looked up into her glittering gold eyes, his own lit with amusement, then he chuckled. 'Nasty, Marlene.'

'Humph,' she snorted inelegantly, crossing to the kitchen sink with her empty cup. 'But probably true, from what I have heard.'

'Your snide comments are not going to deter me, Marlene—and, let's face it, you are hardly in a position to judge the woman.' He had joined her at the sink and, catching her by the arm, he swung her around to face him. 'Let's not pretend you are the injured party in all this. You have done very well out of Rossi over the years. We both know exactly what kind of woman you are. You want money, and I am prepared to see you get a fair settlement.'

His hands slid up her arms and tightened on her shoulders. His closeness, the masculine warmth of him tantalised her senses even as anger at his misguided assumptions about her coloured her cheeks. She glanced helplessly up into his hard face, unable to find a cutting response. His hands caressed her bare arms, raising goosebumps on her over-sensitive skin. She wanted to break away, but her feet seemed glued to the floor. His mouth descended and she waited for his kiss, but instead he continued talking.

'And I can see you get a lot more if you like,' he declared huskily, his mouth brushing her brow. 'I'm also quite prepared to take up where Paolo left off, and keep you as my mistress.' For a stunned moment she was mesmerised by the sensuous invitation in his dark eyes. 'You will find me a very generous lover,' he drawled seductively as his other hand cupped her chin and tilted her head back. 'Both financially and physically, I promise. What do you say?'

Erotic images of his large body, naked and poised over her own, filled Marlene's imagination. She swayed towards him. Then she recognised the triumphant curl of his lip and at the same moment realised that he was going to kiss her. If she let herself be caught in the sexual web the man spun so easily around her she would be no better than what he said she was!

It took every ounce of will-power she possessed to jerk her head free of his hand and take a swift sideways step. Ignoring his crude proposition, she shot across to the door. She turned and leant against the doorframe; she needed the support because her legs were shaking. 'I think you'd better leave, Signor Andretti,' she said bluntly.

'Not the response I expected. But maybe you're right. Best to get all you can from the last love before taking on a new one,' he offered cynically, and in a few lithe strides he had covered the space between them. 'I will call on Thursday for your answer on the shares.'

'You can have it now. No, no and no again.'

'So adamant and so foolish.' His hard eyes sought hers. 'You realise the Rossi family have every right to contest the will in court and stop you getting the villa? They don't have to win—they can tie you up in litigation for years and cost you a fortune. You could end up with nothing at all. Maybe even lose this little business.'

Bravely she held his gaze. 'And you would advise the Contessa to do that, of course.'

'Maybe... Dare you take the chance?' he demanded silkily, giving nothing away.

Perhaps she *was* being foolish. But there was no way she was allowing this man to intimidate her into breaking her promise to Paolo. She had a very personal reason and it was not just for Paul; it was her own private secret.

'Maybe,' she parroted sarcastically. 'But I have no intention of changing my mind. I think we have said all we need to say, so, if you don't mind, I'm tired.' And, turning her back on him, she walked into the hall, intent on getting rid of him.

'But I do mind,' Rocco drawled, and, clasping her around her waist, he spun her to face him. 'I never leave my dates without a goodnight kiss.'

Before Marlene could object, his dark head swooped down and his hard mouth covered hers in a long, drugging kiss. He's doing it again, was her last coherent thought for some time.

'As I thought.' His deep voice rumbled in her ear.

She raised dazed eyes to his. She could feel the pressure of his linked hands at the base of her spine, and a different kind of strictly masculine pressure on her stomach. She licked her lips and felt the swollen contours of her mouth. She should have been disgusted, fighting him off, but all she could feel was the heat of his huge body, the pounding of her blood through her veins, the quivering of every nerve-end under her skin.

'As you thought, what?' she muttered, her passion-clouded eyes drowning in Rocco's glittering black gaze.

'It gets better and better between us with every kiss, every touch. The chemistry is dynamite.' He moved his hips suggestively against her and Marlene bit back a groan. 'We both know it, Marlene. Why deny ourselves?' His lips teased her cheek and one strong hand slid over her hip and down her thigh.

'Deny what?' she mumbled inanely.

'The pleasure we can give each other.' His mouth dropped lower and fastened on her softly parted lips. His tongue traced their swollen fullness with slow eroticism and Marlene's hands linked behind his head as she gave herself up once more to the wonder of his kiss. 'You want me,' he husked against her mouth. 'You ache to feel me buried deep inside you, and I ache to be there.'

In some deep recess of her brain Marlene knew she should deny him, but her body had other ideas. She felt his hand on her naked thigh and the trembling started deep inside her. She felt his long fingers inching higher. She had no idea when he had lifted up her skirt, and didn't really care—until what he was saying registered . . .

CHAPTER FOUR

'FORGET about the past.' His lips trailed kisses around the curve of her jaw. 'Forget about business.' His lips found her neck. 'Forget about the will.' His tongue licked the pulse beating out of control in the hollow of her throat. 'I will take care of everything and make sure you don't lose by it. But first, Marlene—' his dark head lifted '—show me the way to your bedroom, sweetheart.'

An icy tendril of reality pierced her fuddled brain and Marlene tensed in his arms, suddenly aware of the intimacy she was inviting, encouraging a man like Rocco when they were alone in the house. The sensual mist cleared from her golden eyes and she really studied his passion-darkened features.

His jet-black eyes gleamed with lust and a tinge of male triumph. He looked like some big, sleek jungle predator that had just cornered its prey and was anticipating the delight that was to follow. Her arms fell from his neck and she grasped the first thing she could find for protection—the china fruit bowl on the table beside her. Lifting it in her hand, she held it shoulder-high like a shield, apples and oranges cascading around them.

'Let go of me, you great brute, or I'll brain you!' she cried.

An apple bounced off his chest. Rocco automatically let go of her to catch it. He missed!

Marlene had an insane desire to laugh, but choked back the chuckle rising in her throat.

Rocco stepped back, the puzzlement in his eyes a treat to see. He looked at her set face, down at the fruit rolling around the floor, then back to her face. 'You are joking.

Yes?' He shook his head in amazement. 'You have to be. You were with me every step of the way.'

'No.' Forcing down the turbulent emotions flowing through her body and thinking furiously, Marlene continued, 'I simply wanted to see how far you would go to help your clients. It seems even as far as using your body.' The memory of Rocco and Caterina in the garden, planning for him to seduce her, came back to her and gave her the strength to keep her voice reasonably calm. 'Is there a name for a male prostitute?' she queried lightly, while inside she was still shaking.

His black eyes glittered with fury. His face turned red, his big hands reached towards her, curled into fists, then dropped to clench and unclench at his sides. He swore long and violently in his own language—curses that would have made a Naples docker blush.

Marlene had to stifle a gasp of outrage. She dared not let him know she understood. Not yet! Not until she had unravelled the mystery of the crooked share dealings, she told herself firmly. Instead she waited until he finally stopped to draw breath, then commanded bluntly, 'Please just go.'

'Don't worry, I will,' he snarled. 'If you were a man I would have knocked you flat on your back for that insult. But then I should have expected as much from a woman who is only one step up from a prostitute herself.'

'Now who is insulting whom?' Marlene queried cynically.

'Your kind cannot be insulted, and as for helping you with the Contessa—forget I ever said it. Do whatever the hell you want. A bitch like you hasn't a hope of winning against a real lady.' And, swinging on his heel, he pulled open the heavy oak door. 'See you in court!' he flung over his shoulder as he stepped out into the cool night air.

'Italy, yes. Court, never!' Marlene yelled back, unable to contain her anger any longer, and slammed the door behind him.

Trudging upstairs to bed, Marlene couldn't decide whether it was the word 'bedroom' or 'sweetheart' which had brought her back to her senses earlier. Or perhaps, more honestly, the fact that his long fingers had reached the edge of her lace panties had made her panic. She sighed as she walked into her bedroom. Whatever it had been, she doubted she would ever have to fight off the forceful Rocco Andretti's advances again.

Somehow the thought did not give her any satisfaction. She traced her swollen lips with one finger; she could still feel the touch of his mouth on hers. She sighed again with regret. Rocco would be a fantastic lover; the pity of it was she was not likely to find out just how fantastic after tonight's episode...

The captain of the aircraft had kindly allowed the only youngster on the plane to visit the flight deck. Marlene looked up from her magazine and grinned as Paul came running back down the aisle of the aircraft, a stewardess a few steps behind him.

The doubts she had suffered at the thought of Paul's first flight had been dispelled the minute they had reached the airport. The boy had hardly been able to contain his excitement, and a million questions had tumbled from his mouth before they'd even got on the plane. And now, to top it all off, he had actually met the pilot. Her grin broke into a chuckle as he threw himself over her knees to reach his seat by the window, chattering nineteen to the dozen.

'Mar, it was huge—and all lights and sticks and knobs and everything. And I met the pilot and the navi...naval...navig...' The word defeated him. 'And I'm going to be a pilot, Mar.'

Still smiling, Marlene gave him a swift hug. 'I'm sure you will one day, darling.' Reaching across his small body, she fastened his seat belt, and her own. 'But for now, my pet, content yourself with looking out of the window and watching the plane land. We're almost there.'

She had to appear calm and in control for Paul's sake, but inside her stomach was churning with nerves. It wasn't the flight making her nervous, she acknowledged wryly; she actually liked flying; it was the thought of what she had to do in the next few weeks.

The day after her last encounter with Rocco Andretti she had taken a short trip to London and talked to a business associate. The information she had learned was invaluable, and the steps she had put in motion for further information should very quickly succeed.

The following day an official-looking airmail envelope had arrived at her home. Inside had been a rather long-winded letter from the Italian law firm of Andretti, but basically all it had said was that the Contessa would not contest young Paul's right to the villa in Amalfi providing he adhered to the conditions laid down. Paul had to spend two months in Amalfi every year for five years.

But what worried Marlene was the fact that underneath all the legal terminology lay the implication that in return Marlene was to give the Contessa first option on buying her shares in Rossi International and also on buying the villa, if, as Paul's guardian, Marlene decided it would be in his best interest to sell. Also included with the letter had been a map and directions on how to reach the villa, plus the information that the caretaker and his wife would be expecting them.

All very civilised, so why did she have a sneaky suspicion that it was a little *too* civilised? Perhaps the hired help were a pair of psychopaths employed to make their visit so horrible she would be more than grateful to sell the house or, worse, decide never to return to the place, and so the villa would automatically return to the Contessa.

God! She was getting paranoid! Marlene sighed and glanced tenderly down at the small dark head of her brother. In fact, yesterday she had said as much to her own solicitor, and had queried whether it was really worth the bother. She was a wealthy woman in her own right, and of course she would always provide for Paul. But her solicitor had been horrified, and had mentioned the value of the real estate involved as being over two million. His advice was to accept immediately as a prelude to securing young Paul's future.

The seat belt warning lit up in the cabin and Marlene adjusted first Paul's and then her own. The plane was preparing to land. Well, there was no turning back now, she thought resignedly. Let battle commence!

Andretti had been clever and covered all the bases, Marlene thought cynically as the plane touched down, but whether or not he and his friends could disguise the fraud in the Rossi empire so easily remained to be seen. The more she knew of the man, the more convinced she became that Andretti had something to do with the trouble in the late Paolo Rossi's company, and she was determined to find out. Even if it did mean she had to act like a woolly-headed bimbo for a while.

She looked out of the window, her eyes squinting at the glare from the midday sun. So this was southern Italy, she thought wryly, her gaze flickering over Naples airport. She had never been to this part of Italy before. When her mother was alive, Paolo had never wanted to subject her to the animosity of his family here, and had rarely mentioned the place. It had only been after the death of her mother, and with his own health failing, that he had begun to talk about his young son seeing the country of his father's birth.

Marlene smiled as she carried Paul down the aircraft steps, but her golden eyes were hazed with sorrow and she murmured a prayer under her breath. 'Well, Paolo, we're here, Paul and I, as I promised you, and I will try and rescue your company and your good name. May you rest in peace.'

Half an hour later, she walked hand in hand with Paul through the exit gate at Naples airport, and stopped abruptly, her eyes clashing with deep, glittering brown.

'Welcome to Italy, Marlene.' The dark, sexy voice was all too familiar.

She had not been expecting a reception committee, but three feet in front of her stood Rocco Andretti, casually attired in white trousers and a short-sleeved, open-necked silk-knit shirt. There was a sort of dynamic power about him—a vitality that jolted Marlene to the depths of her soul every time she saw him.

Ignoring the frisson of fear—or was it excitement?— that travelled down her spine, and the inexplicable urge to run, she forced her gaze away from him and to the man standing by his side, a very much older man, small, dark and wizened, wearing what looked like a chauffeur's uniform. Her hand tightened on Paul's. Pride and determination to get the better of Andretti gave her the strength to reply in a cool voice.

'Thank you. But there was no need to meet us. The directions were quite explicit.' She straightened her shoulders, adjusting the strap of her bag with her free hand. 'Even I could understand them,' she added with veiled sarcasm. At the same time she was glad she had chosen to wear a plain blue denim skirt and a cropped top for the flight; they reinforced the unsophisticated image she wanted to portray.

'Roc! Roc!' Paul cried. 'I've been on a plane—a huge plane.' And, pulling his hand free of Marlene's, the little boy dashed to the man's side, tugging at his trouser-leg for his attention.

Rocco swooped down and picked Paul up in his arms. 'I know, young man, and judging by the smile on your face you enjoyed it. You can tell me all about the flight in a moment, but first let's get your mum's luggage and get out of here.'

After swinging Paul around once, he deposited him back on the ground. Straightening to his full height, he looked at Marlene, and so missed the puzzled look on the little boy's face and his murmured, 'Mum? But—'

Marlene didn't! She burst into speech. 'Very kind of you, Mr Andretti. So unexpected. Please introduce me to your friend.' And, turning to the little man, she flashed him a brilliant smile. 'I am Marlene Johanson, and this is Paul. Happy to meet you.'

She was gushing but she didn't care. Paul had almost betrayed the fact that she was not his mother, and that was a secret she desperately needed to keep. Italian law was still a mystery to her and, although she was Paul's guardian, his sister Caterina was equally related to him. She was taking no chances on the Rossi family taking Paul over.

The little man broke into a torrent of Italian, all of which Marlene understood perfectly, and she could feel the colour rising in her cheeks at his effusive compliments on her beauty and her marvellous young son. She held out her hand and grasped his nut-brown fingers, and simply continued smiling.

'This is Aldo, the chauffeur-gardener-handyman. His wife is the housekeeper at the villa. Unfortunately neither of them speak much English,' Rocco said smoothly. 'Try saying, *Piacere, Aldo*. That will suffice.' His dark gaze intent on her smiling face, he added, 'Though the way you smiled at him has probably made him your slave for life already. You can't resist ensnaring old men, can you?'

Ignoring Rocco's barbed comment, she slowly repeated the Italian salutation, and was rewarded by a gap-toothed grin from Aldo.

'Let's get in the car before the old fool salivates at your feet,' Rocco said curtly, before instructing Aldo to collect the luggage and meet them outside. Then, catching Marlene by the elbow, and grasping young Paul with his other hand, he almost frogmarched them out of the airport.

The touch of his long fingers on her bare flesh had the same disturbing effect on Marlene as always, and she wanted to pull free. But she thought better of it when she saw the bustle outside. The heat was stifling and the air rang with the sound of arguing and gesticulating Italians. Taxis darted all over, and row upon row of tour buses were lined up, with hundreds of tourists either alighting or embarking.

'Gosh, it's hot, Mar!' Paul exclaimed, his eyes, huge as saucers, darting all over, trying to take in so many new sights and sounds at once.

'It will be much cooler once we get in the car,' Rocco answered him. 'It is air-conditioned.'

As if on cue, a long white Mercedes drew up in front of them with Aldo at the wheel. How had he managed to collect the luggage and fight his way through the traffic in barely five minutes? Marlene could not begin to understand. And as she slid into the back seat of the car, and Rocco slammed the door behind her, she had a sinking sensation that there was an awful lot about the present situation she did not understand. And she was never likely to, if Rocco had his way.

The two-hour car journey was a nightmare. Aldo appeared to be the proof of every bad joke about Italian drivers. He shot out of the car park with a squeal of rubber and Marlene was thrown against Paul, who thought it was hilarious. To Marlene's mind, the only saving grace about the journey was the fact that at least she didn't have to sit beside Rocco. He had taken the front passenger seat and left the back for herself and Paul.

The scenery was magnificent as the road wound around the coast towards Sorrento—cliffs on one side and the deep blue of the Mediterranean on the other. She might have appreciated it, and the couple of gems of information Rocco imparted—pointing out the great health spa hotel and the original Bikini Beach, with its tiny artificial island with one palm tree, equally artificial—except for the fact that Aldo never seemed to have two hands on the wheel at any one time. For some reason he drove in the middle of the road, swerving from every approaching car. On top of that he carried on a non-stop conversation with Rocco on the relative merits of Italian football teams.

When they hit the final leg of the journey along the notorious Amalfi coast road, it took all of Marlene's will-power not to yell at Aldo to slow down. Meanwhile, Paul thought it was brilliant. His nose pressed to the window with childish delight, totally without fear, he described the sheer cliffs falling hundreds of feet to the sea. To Marlene's horror he declared that he felt like a bird and was sure he could fly off them!

It was with a sigh of relief that she recognised they were slowly getting nearer the sea, and when the road finally wound down into Amalfi, and they drove along the harbour of the small port, she finally began to breathe easily again, but not for long...

'Why have we stopped here?' she asked, looking around with interest. There was a small rocky beach and a harbour, where a ferry was just arriving, and on the opposite side of the road were a few shops and terraced houses. 'I don't see a villa here.'

Rocco swung around in his seat, one arm over the back, and grinned. 'The villa is not here. But you need a drink before going any further.'

'Drink? What for?' But she was talking to fresh air. Rocco was out of the car and holding open the door for her.

'Hurry up, Marlene. We'll grab a drink at a café in the square. But we do want to arrive before dark.'

She slid out of the car with more haste than elegance and, leaning back in, lifted Paul out and onto his feet. Keeping a firm grasp on his little hand, she faced up to Rocco.

'What do you mean, *we* have to arrive before dark? Just what are you playing at, Signor Andretti? As far as I am concerned there is no valid reason for you to accompany us at all. And I certainly do not need a drink.' Marlene looked at him coldly, summoning all her strength to meet his dark eyes, and his lips twisted wryly.

'You will! There is a reception committee waiting to meet you, and I thought I'd better give you a few pointers on what is expected of you.'

'What?' she exclaimed in horror. According to the letter she had received, the villa was solely for her and Paul. Now Rocco was saying something quite different.

'Let me explain. The house is about another ten minutes from here, but I thought it would be better for you and Paul if we broke the journey for a while. Aldo can take Paul along the pier to watch the boats dock and we can talk in private over a drink. The Contessa and Caterina are at the villa awaiting your arrival. The Contessa, being the lady she is, decided it was only polite to meet you both and make sure you are comfortable as guests in what is still her house.'

'How very civilised,' Marlene said drily. 'But that still does not explain your presence.'

'As neither of them speaks very good English and you speak no Italian, I will act as interpreter. Break the ice, as I believe you say. Satisfied?' And he smiled, that slow, sexy smile she had seen so many times before.

Marlene was caught by her own deceit. He was right, she thought, swallowing hard. She did need a drink before meeting the female members of the Rossi family. Why did they want to meet her and Paul? In the letter she had received with the directions there had been no mention of the Contessa or Caterina visiting the villa at the same time as herself. It was worrying. Was this their first step in trying to gain control of Paul? Plus, she could not admit to understanding Italian—not yet. So she would have to suffer Rocco's company. Not something she relished, when she only had to look at him to go weak at the knees.

She stared dumbly up at him, noting the glinting triumph behind his grin. She felt trapped, like a mouse by a big cat, tension in every line of her slender body at this new threat. Then suddenly his smile broadened in real humour. His white teeth sparkled against the tanned skin of his face and he reached out to brush a stray tendril of hair from her brow. She shivered and the hard lips quirked.

'I frighten you, Marlene, and I don't see why. I am not threatening to kidnap you, but simply to take you for a drink, give you time to freshen up and then continue our ride.' His deep voice softened. 'And if a different kind of ride appeals to you you only have to ask. I'm your man.'

'You are disgusting,' she said, her face scarlet.

His large hand reached out and caught her slender wrist. 'No, merely stating the obvious when confronted by a beautiful woman.' His lips quirked again. 'Plus, I love teasing you. But come on, we can continue this debate over a glass of wine—or something stronger if you prefer.' And, dropping to his haunches, he ruffled Paul's hair. 'What say you, Paul? Will you go with Aldo to watch the ferry arrive while I talk to your mother? Aldo will buy you an ice cream, OK?'

Paul looked up at Marlene. 'Why does—?'

She just knew he was going to ask, 'Why does he call you my mother?' and, bending down, she did the only thing she could think of to shut him up. She kissed him quickly. 'Do as Rocco says, please, Paul, and we will be back here in...' She glanced sideways at Rocco, who was standing again, and watching her with a rather odd look in his dark eyes.

'Twenty minutes should do it,' Rocco offered.

'See you in twenty minutes,' she said, and, standing up herself, she waited as Rocco explained the arrangement to Aldo. Marlene heaved a sigh of relief when Paul quite happily put his little hand in Aldo's.

Sitting at the roadside café in the centre of Amalfi, she sipped a glass of mellow red wine and gazed in pleasure at the sight before her. On the opposite side of the steeply rising road stood a church, and in keeping with the hilly contours of the place the approach to it was up a vast stone stairway. The steps must run into the hundreds, she mused, and then gasped in delight as the church doors at the top were opened and out came a wedding party.

The stream of guests were all in their very best clothes, the men in dark suits and ties that looked alien to their tanned, weatherbeaten features. The bride was a local girl—Marlene had gathered as much from the conversation of the waiters. The girl looked impossibly young and innocent, dressed in yards and yards of floating white lace, her black hair entwined with flowers and her long veil off her face and trailing behind her as she descended the steps with her new husband.

'Poor fool,' Rocco remarked, with a cynical twist to his hard mouth.

'Why? They make a lovely couple and they look very happy.'

'Surely you're not advocating marriage, Marlene?' he drawled mockingly. 'With your record.'

She shot him an angry glance and took a deep drink of the red wine. What would he know? she thought bitterly. He was the sort of man who took what he wanted where women were concerned, but kept the same hoary old double standard. Showing only contempt for women who did the same. He was such a male chauvinist, and, draining her glass, she could not resist goading him.

'Certainly. I think it's a marvellous institution, and I am actively looking for a husband.' Suddenly she saw an opportunity to put Rocco off pursuing her for good. Let him think she was trawling for a husband and he'd run a mile. So, modifying his words of earlier with 'marriage' instead of 'ride', she continued, 'And if marriage appeals to you you only have to ask.' She licked her full bottom lip with the tip of her tongue and leant slightly towards him. 'I'm your woman.'

He got the connection immediately. '*Touché*, Marlene! But no way!' he shot back.

'Shame.' She sighed in mock sorrow. 'And here was I thinking what excellent husband material you would make—a wealthy lawyer, and you're kind to children and ladies in distress.'

'I doubt you have ever been in distress in your life. The more I see of you, the less I believe you are the blonde airhead you portray. You're much too mercenary and much too good at it,' Rocco opined cynically, his dark eyes narrowing on her lovely face.

Warning bells rang in Marlene's head. She did not like his intense scrutiny or the speculative gleam in his eyes. 'I'm glad to know you think I'm good at something,' she said lightly, and slanted him a flirtatious smile, hoping to divert him. She succeeded ...

'Oh, I know very well your best attribute, Marlene— warming a man's bed. And, as I have mentioned before, I'd be more than happy to make you my mistress—a straightforward, honest relationship. But wife—never. I have yet to see a happy marriage. My own father always had a mistress, and I hate to disillusion you about Rossi, but he had many mistresses before you.'

Marlene knew why, but she was not about to tell Rocco. 'Maybe,' she said, with a negligent toss of her blonde head, and, dropping her voice to a husky murmur, she added outrageously, 'But you have to admit he did save the best till last.' And, pursing her lips, she mouthed a kiss to him.

'God! You're shameless,' Rocco said sternly, but she saw his lips twitch in amusement and the brown eyes glint with humour.

'Unless I miss my guess, exactly how you like your women,' she shot back teasingly.

'And you are *going* to be my woman, Marlene.' He reached across the table and ran a long finger down the soft curve of her cheek, then casually flicked her under the chin. 'And you're going to love every minute—and that's a promise.' His dark eyes met and held hers.

She wanted to deny his comment, but somehow the words would not come. She watched as he raised the glass in his hand and drained the wine, without ever breaking eye contact with her. He held her mesmerised by the sheer force of his piercing gaze. The noise and bustle around them faded into nothing; she was aware only of Rocco—aware with every atom of her being. It was uncanny, magic, and it was only when he placed the glass on the table and turned to signal to the passing waiter that she was able to break free from his sensual spell.

She was frightened . . . For the first time in her life she felt frightened—not of the man, but of herself. She hardly registered his words.

'Now to business. As I told you, the Contessa and Caterina are staying at the villa for a night or two. Until the five years are up, and the villa belongs outright to young Paul, they are perfectly entitled to use it. They are both fine ladies and expect a certain standard of behaviour. The Contessa is being very brave and generous in even meeting you, considering your position in her late husband's life, so I expect you to try and behave like a lady.'

That did register. 'Behave like a lady'? Of all the cheek. Marlene could not believe what she was hearing. Her would-be Latin lover of a minute ago was actually lecturing her on how to behave.

'I know you're not used to this sort of society, but really all you need to remember is basic good manners.'

If Marlene had not been sitting down she would have fallen down. So this was what he'd meant by giving her 'a few pointers', she thought, suddenly furious. 'You mean like not eating off my knife or slurping the soup or—horror of horrors—blowing my nose on my napkin,' she snarled, and, pushing her chair back, got to her feet. 'Keep your pointers, buster. It will be a cold day in hell before I need a lecherous lout like you to teach me manners.' And, shooting him a vitriolic look, she added, 'I'm going to find Paul. As for you—you can go to hell.'

She only managed half a dozen steps before Rocco grabbed her arm and spun her around to face him.

'That is just the kind of behaviour I was trying to warn you about. I don't give a damn how you eat, you stupid bitch,' he grated in a low, hard voice, 'but you will treat the Contessa and Caterina with the respect they deserve. Got that?' He shook her arm, as if to reinforce his command. His brown eyes glittered angrily down into hers. 'And if you have any sense at all in your admittedly lovely head you'll take my advice, accept the Contessa's offer for the shares and the villa, go back to England and forget you ever knew anyone named Rossi.'

'Let go of my arm and keep your advice to yourself,' Marlene said flatly, but inside she was seething with anger and deep-down disappointment. With his words he had proved what she had thought all along. He might tease her about wanting her, about being her lover, but the bottom line was that he was really only interested in getting the Contessa what she wanted. And if he could get Marlene to agree he would have her on the next flight out of Naples without a backward glance...

CHAPTER FIVE

THE last few miles of the journey passed in a red haze for Marlene; she saw nothing of the countryside, she was so furious. Luckily Paul had dozed off in the back seat, his little head nestling on Marlene's lap. She looked down at him and gradually her anger dissipated and her usual good humour reappeared. With it, she became aware of the irony of her situation. She should be flattered, she told herself. Here she was, an intelligent, well-educated, wealthy woman in her own right, and yet apparently she had played the part of sexy but brainless mistress so well that even the astute Andretti had been fooled enough to break their journey and give her a lesson in manners!

The car stopped and Paul woke up with a start. Sliding along the seat to look out of the window, he demanded, 'Are we there?'

'It would seem so, darling,' she murmured, glancing out of the window at the huge iron gates blocking the road in front of the car.

The heavy gates swung open, obviously electrically operated, and the car moved slowly forward up a steep gradient. Marlene looked around with interest. They were moving up a long drive shrouded on each side by massive conifers, then suddenly the road swept around a bend and before them was the most unusual house Marlene had ever seen.

The sun, sinking low in the sky, bathed the brilliant white and glass structure in a rosy pink glow, and the rays reflecting back dazzled the onlooker, giving it an almost surreal appearance. Somehow she had been expecting a traditional Mediterranean-style villa. Instead, the house was starkly modern—all angles and straight lines.

The entrance door, patterned glass set in a soaring glass pyramid reminiscent of Pei's glass structures outside the Louvre in Paris, was joined on one side to a stark, white-walled flat-roofed structure that slanted to the ground at a sharp angle with not another window in sight. The phrase 'blot on the landscape' sprang to mind. It might have been the set for a science fiction movie set on an alien planet. Marlene could not connect the building with what she knew of the Contessa and her daughter—or Paolo, for that matter.

He had never talked much about his life in Italy, other than to explain about his failed marriage, and he had certainly never mentioned a house in Amalfi. It had come as a complete surprise to Marlene to discover after his death that he had left the villa to his son. True, he had requested she take young Paul to Italy, but she had simply assumed he meant her to take the boy on holiday—stay in a hotel or something. He had never once so much as hinted that he was going to make the request official in his Will. In a way she was a little hurt that Paolo had not confided in her completely. No, that was not strictly true. She took a deep, sighing breath. The personal letter he had left for her to read after his death had told her more than she really wanted to know...

The car door swung open. 'You look stunned.' Rocco's voice broke into her disturbed thoughts. 'Not what you expected?' He smiled down into her golden eyes. 'Quite a revelation, hmm?'

If only he knew, she thought drily. The house was nothing compared to the revelation Paolo had imparted to her in his letter. Still, she pinned a smile on her face and said, 'Yes, quite a revelation.' And, swinging her legs to the ground, she stood up, adding, 'It looks new.' She would have said more, but Paul had slid out behind her and, quick as a flash, was heading for the plain white marble steps up to the entrance. 'Wait, Paul.' She hurried after him and together they arrived on the top step just as the glass door swung open.

Bending to catch Paul, she froze and looked up into the face of Caterina. But she was not looking at Marlene. All her attention was centred on Rocco.

Marlene straightened up to her full height and it suddenly struck her that so much glass around a young child was not the safest thing in the world. So, bending again, she scooped Paul up in her arms. It was just as well she had, because for a moment it hid her scarlet face from Rocco. Scarlet because she had just heard Caterina's greeting to the man and was once again furious.

After the usual pleasantries Caterina had added, 'Pity you couldn't have got rid of the peasant and her brat on the way up, and save us all a lot of trouble and money.' And then she had laughed.

Marlene, holding Paul in front of her like a shield, straightened to her full height, this time looking down on Caterina, and she could not resist saying, *'Buena sera, Caterina*. I hope that was right—I've been reading an Italian phrase book.' She was so caught up in her own anger she did not see the sudden sharp glance Rocco shot her way, or the glint of suspicion in his dark eyes.

The next half-hour was hell! More than once Marlene had to clench her teeth to restrain herself from commenting, and if it had not been for her promise to Paolo she would have turned around and walked out.

Caterina led them all through the glass foyer and down a massive marble staircase into what was obviously a kind of formal reception room. Rocco briefly explained on the way down the stairs that they had entered by what was really the back of the house, onto the top floor. The staircase curved to one side and carried on down a further three floors. There was also a lift for those who preferred it. The middle two floors housed the bedrooms, and the ground floor contained a more informal salon, a dining room and study, plus the usual kitchen and utility rooms, and a small family room that led directly onto a wide terrace and the swimming pool.

He stopped abruptly as they entered the room, and a petite, flamboyantly dressed lady rose from a white hide armchair and simply stood in the middle of the room. The Contessa was everything Marlene had feared and more.

Rocco strolled over and kissed the woman on both cheeks before commanding Marlene and Paul to come along and be introduced. Five minutes later they were all seated like stuffed dummies around the lady of the house. The usual polite greetings were exchanged, with Rocco translating all the time. But what really made Marlene's blood boil was the way he translated.

He translated the usual social pleasantries accurately, but he omitted the most telling part of the Contessa's speech. In a scathing aside to Rocco, she said, 'The boy I can see is certainly Rossi's son—he has the same coarse features. No doubt a blood test will prove the relationship. As for the woman,' she said scathingly, 'you...' And then she hesitated, turning her gimlet black eyes on Marlene, coldly assessing. Then, as if she had thought better of insulting Marlene, she continued, 'No, it doesn't matter—not now. I need to think.'

At that point a pleasant-looking woman introduced as Eta, the chauffeur's wife, arrived with a tea-tray laden with small sandwiches, scones and cakes, plus teapot and cups, of course. According to Rocco, this was supposedly in honour of the English guests. Marlene burned from red to white with anger. She drank the tea and ate a scone, and was grateful when Paul declared he had eaten enough, he was tired and wanted to go to bed. Pinning a smile on her face, she excused them both and followed Eta down to the next floor and the rooms allocated to them.

Standing at the large window, staring out at the now dark sky, Marlene sighed dispiritedly. Paul, after very little fuss, was safely in bed in what was the dressing room of her room. His day was over. But for her, she had no doubt, worse was to come. 'Dinner at nine,' were the last words Rocco had said to her. She had not looked at him but had simply said yes as she'd led Paul away from the adults. Alone at last, the enormity of the task she had taken on was beginning to hit her.

In some respects the Contessa had come as something of a shock. In Marlene's mind she had pictured a middle-aged lady, very formal, very conservative. But the woman was nothing like that. Small and quite attractive, she couldn't be more than forty-five and might easily pass for thirty-five. Her clothes were designer label—Versace, probably—brightly coloured and quite avant-garde. But the eyes gave her away. She was very like her daughter, but whereas Caterina's dark eyes were easily readable, showing all her emotions, the mother's were the opposite, showing no emotion even when she smiled. There was a hardness, a guarded, almost cunning look about the woman that made Marlene shiver just to think about it.

Suddenly chilled, although the temperature outside must have been in the nineties, Marlene turned away from the window and walked quickly across the room to the *en suite* bathroom. She was being fanciful, she told herself. A nice long soak in the bath and she would feel much better.

Fifteen minutes later, stretched out in the luxurious tub, which was filled to the brim with warm water and a fragrant layer of bubbles, Marlene closed her eyes and let her mind drift. It had been a fraught five days since that fateful afternoon when Rocco Andretti and Caterina had appeared in the herb garden and she had decided to play the part of Paul's mother.

Looking back, she realised it had been the behaviour of the other couple that had goaded her into it, but realistically she knew she was not going to be able to keep it up for very much longer. Twice already young Paul had almost given her away; it was only a matter of time before the truth came out. She had panicked when she'd overheard Caterina and Rocco discussing getting control of the boy, when in reality they had no chance. After all, she was Paul's legal guardian and as closely related as Caterina—plus, she had the added advantage of having always looked after the boy.

Picking up a bar of soap, she raised one leg and began to wash herself. Yes, she decided, it didn't matter if the truth came out. In fact she would tell them all after dinner tonight. Her mind was made up. Briskly she completed her ablutions, not once admitting even deep down that her decision had more to do with letting Rocco know she was not the immoral woman he thought, but simply a caring young woman looking after her brother, than with a desire to tell the truth.

Dried and dusted, Marlene walked back into the bedroom. Her suitcase had been brought up earlier by Aldo and unpacked by Eta, she presumed as she slid back the wardrobe door. Oh, no! She eyed the few clothes and could have wept. The day before leaving England she had shopped at one of the high-street stores for clothes that would fit the image she was hoping to portray, and, looking at them now, she realised she was stuck with it. She could reveal the truth of her relationship with Paul all right, but until the day of the board meeting she was still going to have to appear in clothes she would never ordinarily have bought.

She withdrew a bright yellow jersey silk dress and sighed, thinking longingly of her wardrobe at home. What wouldn't she give for her favourite Calvin Klein peach silk trouser suit? But it was her own stupid fault and she would have to make the best of it.

Five minutes later, as she surveyed her reflection in the full-length mirror, she groaned. It was a simple mini-skirted slip dress—apparently all the rage! With tiny shoestring straps and a deep, curved neckline showing a great deal of cleavage, the jersey silk skimmed her hips to end at mid-thigh. At five feet nine she should have remembered exactly how short a normal mini-length garment would appear on her. She tugged and tugged at the skirt, hoping to stretch it, and finally gave up, resigned to the fact that no amount of tugging at the thing was going to make it any longer.

Quickly she applied a minimum of make-up to her face—a moisturiser and sweep of translucent powder that allowed her naturally golden skin to show through. She paid a little more attention to her eyes, brushing the lids with a beige-brown eyeshadow and accentuating them with a fine light brown line and a few sweeps of brown-black mascara to her long lashes. She coloured her full lips with a soft rose lipstick and was almost ready. She brushed her long hair until it shone and fastened it behind her ears with two gilt combs. After slipping her feet into flat gold pumps, as a final touch she sprayed her throat and behind her knees with her favourite perfume, Dune. Then, straightening up, she headed for the door.

But just as she reached it somebody knocked. Turning the handle, she pulled it open and stared...

'Waiting for my knock, were you?' Rocco asked flippantly. 'I'm flattered.'

Marlene was speechless. She'd known he was handsome, but in a formal white dinner jacket he was devastating!

'Cat got your tongue?' he drawled huskily, his eyes appreciating every exposed inch of her with bold, sensual delight. 'Try mine instead.'

Before she could utter a word he had pulled her into his arms, and his mouth caught and clung to hers as he kissed her with a passion and intensity that made her legs buckle. His tongue plunged into her mouth and she met him with equal intensity, her body pressed against his hard frame, her breasts tingling with the contact.

Rocco finally raised his head, breaking the kiss. His breathing unsteady, he stared down into her flushed, confused face. 'My God!' he muttered. 'I can almost understand Rossi throwing away his life for you. You're incredible.' And, as he held her away from him, his smouldering dark eyes swept down over the proud jut of her breasts against the fine fabric.

'Paolo...' She was going to tell him the truth but she never got the chance.

'Stop,' he said fiercely, hauling her back against him. 'Don't dare say that name when you are in my arms. I won't have it,' he snarled, and, his eyes glittering with anger, his mouth clamped on hers once again. But this kiss was different—hard and ruthless, seeking no response, simply dominating.

Frantically Marlene pushed against his broad chest, fighting to break free. She twisted her head away from him. 'No!' she cried. 'Leave me alone!'

'I wish to God I could,' Rocco growled, suddenly setting her free. 'There is something between us—we only have to touch each other to go up in flames. You can't deny it, so why bother trying?'

Marlene looked up into his darkly flushed face, her heart racing crazily, and knew what he said was true. 'But you don't understand...' Again she tried to tell him the truth, and again he stopped her.

'What's to understand?' he rasped, his voice hoarse. 'I want you. I've got to have you or go insane. I'm a wealthy man—I can give you anything you want. All you have to do is agree to be my mistress.'

She shook her head, still half-dazed by his kisses, and pushed out of his arms, trying to think. 'But what about the reason why I'm here?' They were fated to be enemies, however much Marlene wished it could be otherwise.

Rocco's hands closed over her naked shoulders and held her steady. 'No. Wait—listen. I'm not asking for for ever,' he said urgently. 'Only for a few weeks or months—whatever it takes until this fever between us burns itself out naturally. Forget about the rest. Business has nothing to do with pleasure.'

Her golden eyes widened in horror as the realisation of what he was saying hit her like a bucket of cold water. She stared at him as her heartbeat slowed and a cold fury took the place of her former mindless passion. He had just thoroughly insulted her.

'I don't believe you,' she drawled, shaking her head at the sheer arrogance of the man. But obviously his English was not as good as she had thought, because he took what she had said literally, missing the sarcasm completely.

'I'm telling you the truth—believe me. I'll take care of you and the boy, and to prove it we will leave here tomorrow. I have a place a few miles from here. It is yours if you want it. Simply let me have you.'

Her mouth tightened into an angry, bitter line and, stepping back, she roughly pushed his hands from her shoulders. 'Get out, before I scream,' she grated between clenched teeth. It was all clear to her now. 'We will leave here tomorrow' he had said. How very convenient for the Contessa and her daughter if Rocco succeeded in his plan to seduce her into leaving with him. Obviously Paul would go with them, and his inheritance would also go—straight down the drain. Rocco must think she was a complete idiot.

Rocco stared at her, his dark eyes narrowed in speculation. 'What is it I'm missing here? You melt in my arms, then threaten to scream after I've offered you anything you like.' He moved towards her but she sidestepped him.

'Perhaps I just don't like you, Signor Andretti,' she said bluntly. 'Now please leave. I need to repair my make-up and check on Paul before going down to dinner.'

He watched her for a long, silent moment, the tension stretching between them tight as a bowstring. 'I do not understand you at all. You are beautiful, basic, but there is something about you that doesn't add up...' He turned away from her with a frustrated shake of his dark head. 'We haven't time to talk now. I'll wait outside. I originally came to show you the way to the dining room and I still intend to.' And with that he was gone, the door closing quietly behind him.

Marlene took a few deep, steadying breaths. Her act was definitely slipping; he was suspicious. Her decision to tell him the truth of her relationship with Paolo was the right one. As soon as she could get him alone she would do it, then perhaps the relationship between them could develop honestly. The thought made her smile and, after quickly tidying her hair and replacing her vanished lipstick, she took a brief look at Paul before eagerly opening the bedroom door.

Rocco was waiting, leaning negligently against the wall. 'You surprise me. I thought it would take you at least another ten minutes—not because your beauty needs assistance but simply to keep me waiting. That is the usual women's ploy, I've found.'

'You obviously meet the wrong type of women,' Marlene snapped, her good humour vanishing at the thought of all his other women. She would have walked past him, but he caught her arm and, straightening to his full height, stared down into her mutinous face.

'*You* certainly are,' he muttered with some exasperation, before gently nudging her before him. 'Come on, the Contessa does not like to be kept waiting.'

The dining room was weird, Marlene thought as Rocco pulled out a black and glass chair for her, and she sat down, glancing around curiously. A huge plate-glass wall opened out onto a large patio lit with a row of sharply angled halogen lights that gave an eerie white glare, making the blackness beyond impenetrable. She imagined that in the daylight the view must be quite spectacular, but at the moment all she could see was some patio furniture and some potted cactus plants. Not a flower or rambling hibiscus in sight, yet it matched the rest of the place.

The dining room itself contained only a twelve-foot long black marble table and eleven more black and glass chairs like the rather uncomfortable one she was sitting on. A huge modern sculpture that must have been about nine feet high took up one wall where, in a more conventional house, one might have expected a fireplace. The few pictures on the other two walls were very Salvador Dali and quite possibly originals, but they were not really to Marlene's taste.

The lighting came from a selection of long black standard lamps with strange white globes which lit the ceiling rather than the table, and in the centre of the table was yet another sculpture—at least, Marlene supposed it was a sculpture—all stainless steel and wire but surprisingly functional as it held twelve black candles. The whole effect was theatrical, and to her mind chilling.

Even more chilling were her dinner companions. They were four in all and the other two females were already seated. The Contessa, at the head of the table, spoke first.

'We were beginning to think you had gone.'

Marlene's head jerked up. The woman spoke English. 'You speak English,' she said, surprised, and flashed a quick glance at Rocco. He did not look in the least surprised. So much for his need to be here and translate. The liar, she thought cynically. But she made no comment, turning her attention back to the Contessa as that lady continued.

'A little, but not so good. This—' she indicated the small, heavy man standing at her right-hand side '—is Signor Andretti—Rocco's *papà*.' And she smiled, a thin twist of her lips. 'And Caterina you know.' She glanced at her daughter, seated one place away, as the older man also sat down next to her.

Marlene sensed Rocco's hands tighten on the back of her chair, before he apparently casually pulled out the chair beside her and sat down.

'I did not expect you to be here so soon, Papà,' Rocco said in Italian, and Marlene picked up the tension between the two men immediately.

'Rocco, please—we try to talk English for our visitor, no?' the Contessa intervened, with a blatantly false smile for Marlene.

The dinner went from bad to worse. The food was excellent, but there were so many undercurrents it made Marlene's head spin. That, together with the knowledge that she was sitting here supposedly as a dead man's mistress, and they were all being so terribly sophisticated and civilised about it, made her feel slightly sick. Not for the first time she wondered if fulfilling Paolo's last wish was really worth the aggravation. Added to all this, the difficulty she had in pretending she did not speak their language was a terrible strain, as the conversation constantly switched from English to Italian, depending on who was talking.

It was after the dessert had been eaten—a rather luscious concoction of nuts, strawberries and cream and various flavoured ice creams—that the bomb fell.

'So, Marlene,' the Contessa said silkily as the dessert dishes were taken away, 'who are you? You are not my husband's woman; this I know...'

Marlene's eyes widened in shock as they met the narrowed gaze of the Contessa. What did the woman mean? Did she know the truth? The questions spun in her brain. Then, remembering her decision taken earlier in the bedroom to come clean, she opened her mouth to speak. But she was too late. Rocco intervened.

'Really, Contessa, we all know the circumstances. I don't think we need to embarrass Miss Johanson.' He cast a sideways glance at Marlene, sitting next to him.

If he thought his smile was reassuring, Marlene thought bitterly, he was wrong. She was not an idiot. His lips might tilt at the corners, but his dark eyes held an unmistakably cynical gleam.

The Contessa shot him an exasperated glance and let fly in rapid Italian. 'Rocco, if you spent less time with your head in the ground and more in the real world you would not be so easily fooled by a pretty face. And as for you, Caterina, you are no better. The woman has fooled you both. My late husband's mistress was the same age as me, for God's sake!' And then, turning, she laid her hand on the other Andretti's arm. 'I warned you, Carlo. You should have gone yourself to England, not sent Rocco.'

Andretti senior let fly with a barked question. 'Surely you had the sense to check the woman out, Rocco?'

His response was lost in Caterina's cry. 'Of course she's the one!'

Marlene would have found the following slanging match quite funny if it had not been her they were talking about. Finally there was silence, and four pairs of eyes fixed on Marlene with various expressions.

Caterina sat in open-mouthed amazement, her mother in glittering triumph and the senior Andretti regarded her with shrewd dark eyes. Oddly enough, Marlene realised, the man was nothing like his son. Where Rocco was very tall, lean and muscular, this man, she judged, was not above five feet seven. His face was round, his nose large and his eyes small, and he was definitely over-weight. Perhaps Rocco took after his mother, she mused, but was rudely brought back to the question at hand when she finally turned her head to Rocco, at her side.

'The Contessa asked you a question, Miss Johanson,' he grated scathingly from between clenched teeth, his dark eyes blazing with anger, his hard mouth a tight line. 'Now answer it...'

'What was the question again?' she asked blandly, playing for time. 'You all started talking at once.' She shrugged. 'Not that I understood a word.'

'Who exactly are you, Marlene?'

She pushed her chair back and slowly got to her feet, her mind working like lightning. Just how much was it safe to reveal? she wondered. But Rocco, mistaking her action as an attempt to leave, leapt to his feet and placed a firm, restraining hand on her shoulder.

'No, you are not walking out on this, lady. No one makes a fool of me and gets away with it. Just who the hell are you?' he said in a deadly voice, the other people in the room forgotten. 'You either answer to me or to the police.'

'Police!' she exclaimed in astonishment, glancing up into his angry face.

'Fraud is a serious offence.' His eyes duelled with hers, implacable, black as jet and just as cold.

'You should know.' She tried to sneer, but the pressure of his hand on her shoulder increased until it physically hurt her.

His father interrupted. 'Let the lady speak.'

As if suddenly realising there were other people present, Rocco allowed his hand to fall from her shoulder. 'Well, Marlene?'

The moment of truth had arrived. Or partial truth, she qualified silently. Taking a deep, slow breath, resting her hands lightly on the back of the chair she had just vacated, she turned all her attention on the Contessa. 'I am Marlene Johanson—the Marlene Johanson mentioned in your late husband's will as his son's guardian. You can check it and you will find it is all perfectly legal.

I am Paul's legal guardian but I was never your husband's mistress. My mother was. She died two years ago.'

'The boy calls you Ma,' Rocco sneered. 'Maybe Rossi went from mother to daughter.'

Without a second thought Marlene swung her hand through the air and slapped him soundly in the face, knocking his head back with the force of the blow. She vaguely heard the gasps of outrage from the rest of the table but she was past caring. This man had insulted her once too often.

Before he could recover she was out of the door and racing up the stairs to her room. The door safely locked behind her, she leant against it and tried to recover her breath and her temper. God knew what the rest of them thought. That she was crazy, probably.

A few moments later, when she had finally calmed down enough to think straight, she realised that her show of violence might have harmed her case for keeping young Paul—if the Rossi family decided to make a case of it. But on the other hand she had something they wanted even more—the shares in the Rossi empire—so perhaps all was not lost, she mused as she slid gratefully into the wide bed.

A quick glance at the headboard was not reassuring; it was a curved black railing topped with gilded spikes. Her last thought before sleep finally overcame her was that she did not like the house or the décor, never mind the inhabitants... She didn't hear the soft tap on the door, or the deep voice whispering her name over and over again with rising masculine frustration...

CHAPTER SIX

'MAR, wake up—wake up!' Marlene groaned and gripped the little hand pounding on her chest. 'Not there, Paul, that hurts.' Forcing her eyes open, she looked up into the grinning face of her brother. His black hair was all awry and his pyjama jacket had disappeared. Clad only in Batman-printed pyjama bottoms, he sat astride her waist, his little hands pressing on her chest and his face only inches from hers.

'You're awake. You've got to see. Come on—quick.' His excitement was infectious.

'What have I got to see?' Marlene queried, hauling herself up the bed and depositing Paul on the floor at the same time.

'The sea and the cliffs, Mar. I've never seen such big cliffs. And a swimming pool and the sun.'

'OK, OK.' And, swinging her legs over the side of the bed, she stood up, and put her hands above her head, stretching and yawning at the same time. Paul was already standing with his face pressed up to the window as Marlene, with a wry smile at his early morning enthusiasm, strolled over to join him. Resting her hand on his little shoulder, she followed his gaze. He was right, she thought wonderingly. In daylight the view was spectacular.

The cloudless sky blended into the sea at the horizon, a deep clear blue, and, closer, the water changed to a vivid aquamarine, with dark rocks and vegetation clearly visible beneath the surface. The house itself appeared to be carved into the soaring cliffs. Looking immediately down, she saw the patio that ran the length of the villa, and a diamond-shaped swimming pool sparkling clear jade in the morning sun. Then several steep terraces ran down in layers for about five hundred yards, before appearing to fall into the sea.

The drop down the cliff must be astronomical, she thought, going by the distance to the next view of the rocks as the sea lapped at their base. Again it occurred to her that the house had not been planned with children in mind. Paul would need watching like a hawk for however long they stayed here. The steps were too steep for a young child, and there was not a guard rail in sight.

'Can I go in the pool, Mar?' Paul asked, tugging at the hem of her short cotton nightie.

'Yes, come on, pet. I'll get you washed.'

'But I don't need a wash—the pool will wash me.'

There was no answer to that, so Marlene simply picked him up and carried him into the bathroom.

Ten minutes later, with Paul dressed in his swimming trunks and a T-shirt, leaping up and down with impatience by the bedroom door, Marlene pulled a loose knee-length cotton jersey sweater dress over her white Lycra bathing suit, picked up a towel and glanced ruefully at her watch on the bedside table. Seven a.m. Still, she thought bracingly, a few lengths of the pool would do her the world of good, and maybe help her get her thoughts in order.

Opening the bedroom door, she ushered Paul out, with a finger to her lips to remind him to be quiet. She very much doubted if the other members of the household would be awake this early.

In that she was mistaken. Quietly she led Paul downstairs and in a false start opened a door to what was obviously a study. She shut it again. Her next attempt revealed the kitchen, where Eta and Aldo were seated at a hideous—to Marlene's eyes—stainless-steel table, enjoying a pot of coffee.

'*Scusi, signorina*—you should have rung.' Eta jumped to her feet. 'It is my duty to bring you your morning coffee and breakfast,' she said in rapid Italian, with a look of dismay clouding her pleasant features.

Marlene smiled and responded quietly in the same language. 'It's perfectly all right. We're going for a swim—coffee and juice will do fine, thank you.' The wide grin that spread over Eta's features alerted Marlene to her mistake.

'Yes, immediately, *signorina*,' Eta said.

With an inward groan Marlene realised that, still not properly awake, she had rattled off her statement in Italian. She toyed with the idea of trying to explain to Eta that she wanted to keep her linguistic ability a secret, but quickly discarded the notion. She had no idea how close the woman was to her employer, and she might just make matters worse. Instead she took the cup of coffee Eta handed her, and drank it quickly while Paul swallowed down a large glass of fresh orange juice. Then, with a simple nod of her head and a smile, she hurried Paul out through the kitchen and onto the patio.

The morning air was warm but fresh, and Marlene took great gulps into her lungs. She felt as though she had been confined for ages, what with the plane journey and the car journey yesterday, and then the disastrous evening. But outside in the clear air, with the sound of the sea splashing against the rocks the only noise, at last she felt a sense of freedom. With Paul's hand firmly clasped in her own she led him along the terrace to where the swimming pool sparkled in the sun.

Sitting on a convenient lounger, she quickly divested Paul of his T-shirt and herself of the sweater dress, then gingerly walked to the edge of the glistening pool.

'Now, wait there and don't move until I come back and lift you into the water. Promise?'

'But why, Mar?'

'Because there are no markings and I have to find out which is the safest part.'

'But I can swim.'

'Don't argue,' she said, and, dropping the towel on the ground, added firmly, 'Wait.'

It was as she had suspected, she found, after a speedy crawl around the pool. There was no part shallow enough for Paul to stand up in. Hauling herself out of the pool beside him, she led him to the point of the diamond that faced out to sea. Here the water was four feet deep; the boy would not be able to stand, but she felt he might be marginally safer.

Ten minutes later, standing up to her chest in the water, she brushed the wet hair out of her eyes and picked Paul out of the water by the armpits and swung him around. 'Tired yet, darling?' she asked, laughing. He was a great little swimmer—she had taught him herself—but there was only so much a boy of his age could do. 'Come on, sit on the side and rest for a second.' Lowering him onto the edge, so that only his feet dangled in the water, she turned and pushed herself up to sit beside him. 'Do you think you would like to stay here?' she asked quietly, and, picking up the towel, she rubbed the black curls on the top of his head.

'That is a leading question if ever I heard one,' a deep voice commented. Marlene got such a shock that she slid back into the pool, and Rocco's shout of laughter did nothing for her temper.

But Paul had no such trouble. He jumped to his feet and spun around, racing across the terrace to where Rocco stood at the top of the steps. 'Roc! I've been swimming—did you see me? Did you?'

'Yes, you were great—and so was your mother.'

'Not mother, silly. Marlene's my sister.'

The conversation was lost to Marlene. She was too busy hauling herself back out of the pool again, the dripping towel still in her hand. Trust him to be up at the crack of dawn, she thought resentfully. He must have been down at the bottom terrace before they'd come out of the house. Leaving the towel on the ground—it was useless now—she stood up. Catching her hair in a bunch, she wrung the excess moisture out of it, before straightening and looking across at her tormentor.

He had dropped to his knees to talk to Paul, and she had time to study him. Rocco was wearing brief black bathing shorts and, apart from a white towel slung around his neck, nothing much else except for a pair of black rubber flip-flops on his feet. A sudden coil of attraction twisted to life in the pit of her stomach at the sight of his tanned legs with their light dusting of black body hair. The graceful curve of his broad, tanned back made her itch to run a finger down his spine.

He turned suddenly. 'Good morning, Marlene. You're looking well.' Rocco rose to his full height and quite deliberately let his eyes roam over her from head to toe in a sensuous appraisal that made her one-piece suit suddenly seem too small and too tight.

The colour surged into her cheeks. But she said very curtly, 'Good morning and goodbye,' to some point over his left shoulder. 'Come on, Paul, time for breakfast.' And, stepping forward, she reached out her hand to Paul. But he was not so easily persuaded.

'No, Mar. Me and Roc are going to swim.'

Grasping Paul's hand firmly in her own, she tilted her head back and forced herself to look at Rocco. 'It is time for his breakfast. Perhaps later,' she said bluntly.

His black eyes narrowed on her flushed face. 'Too late, Marlene—or should I call you Mar, like your brother?' he drawled sardonically.

The anger of last night was still very evident. She might have guessed he would not let her off lightly for pretending to be Rossi's mistress and making a fool of him in front of his father and the Contessa. 'Call me what you like. I'm sure you can think of a few choice names.'

She tried to joke, hoping he would put her heightened colour down to amusement, when really she was deeply embarrassed by the way she had behaved—or perhaps, more honestly, by being found out in a lie.

'You have a good reason to blush, after last night,' Rocco taunted cynically. 'I'm only amazed your nose hasn't grown a foot long, you devious little liar.'

'You believed what you wanted to believe. I can't help it if you have a mind like a sewer,' she shot back defensively.

'Why, you—' His black eyes glittered with fury and she instinctively took a step back, but before he could say anything more Paul saved her.

'Mar, are you and Roc fighting?'

'No,' she snapped, and, instantly regretting her sharp response, she gently squeezed Paul's hand and smiled down at him. 'No, darling. Sorry, it's just a slight disagreement. You can swim again later. Now come on.'

Paul recognised that she was serious by the tone of her voice and made no more attempt to argue. Instead he quite happily skipped along beside her as she turned around and strode back towards the house, calling over his shoulder, 'See you later, Roc. I'm hungry now.'

She heard a splash behind her and guessed that Rocco had dived into the pool. Probably to cool off; he had looked absolutely furious.

Marlene had to hide her own fury a few minutes later when, on walking into the kitchen, she was accosted by the Contessa.

'Breakfast is taken alfresco, at nine. Time for you and the child to dress,' she said with a disdainful look at Marlene and Paul's scantily clad bodies. 'I preserve a certain standard always.'

'Of course,' Marlene mumbled, and dashed Paul back upstairs as quickly as she could, thinking all the while that there was no way she could stand living in this house with that woman for two weeks, never mind two months.

By the time breakfast was over, she had amended the thought from two weeks to two days, having remembered that Rocco had said she and Caterina were only staying a night or two. The Contessa and Andretti senior had sat together, whispering all the time. Caterina had not appeared, and Rocco had sat in a brooding silence, watching every movement Marlene made. In the end she'd barely eaten a thing, she was so disconcerted. Only young Paul seemed oblivious of the tension in the air, and munched his way through a bowl of cornflakes and a plate of scrambled eggs, finally declaring that he was full and asking what they were going to do next. Marlene felt like saying, Leave...

It was almost a relief when the Contessa commanded her to meet her in the study in fifteen minutes.

'Yes, but what about Paul? This is not the safest place to allow a child to run around in,' Marlene responded evenly. She had no intention of allowing the Contessa to order her about.

'I will look after Paul,' Rocco said smoothly. 'So you can concentrate on the business at hand.'

Marlene cast a time-wasting glance around the terrace, but eventually she had to look at him—something she had been studiously avoiding for the past half-hour, although she had been intensely aware of him every second. Her golden eyes, narrowed against the sun, met and clashed with his. There was a stillness, a waiting about him that she found terribly threatening even as her body acknowledged her sensual awareness of him with rapidly beating heart.

'You can trust me with him, Marlene,' he said, not taking his eyes from her face. 'I will look after him.'

'How very noble of you. Thank you,' she said sarcastically. But who was going to look after her? she pondered as she slid back her chair and got to her feet.

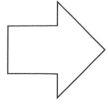

NO COST! NO OBLIGATION TO BUY!
NO PURCHASE NECESSARY!

PLAY "LUCKY 7" AND GET FIVE FREE GIFTS!

HOW TO PLAY:

1. With a coin, carefully scratch off the silver box at the right. Then check the claim chart to see what we have for you—FREE BOOKS and a gift—ALL YOURS! ALL FREE!

2. Send back this card and you'll receive brand-new Harlequin Presents® novels. These books have a cover price of $3.50 each, but they are yours to keep absolutely free.

3. There's no catch. You're under no obligation to buy anything. We charge nothing—ZERO—for your first shipment. And you don't have to make any minimum number of purchases—not even one!

4. The fact is thousands of readers enjoy receiving books by mail from the Harlequin Reader Service®. They like the convenience of home delivery...they like getting the best new novels BEFORE they're available in stores...and they love our discount prices!

5. We hope that after receiving your free books you'll want to remain a subscriber. But the choice is yours—to continue or cancel, anytime at all! So why not take us up on our invitation, with no risk of any kind. You'll be glad you did!

THIS SURPRISE MYSTERY GIFT CAN BE YOURS _FREE_ AS ADDED THANKS FOR GIVING OUR READER SERVICE A TRY!

PLAY "LUCKY 7"

**Just scratch off the silver box with a coin.
Then check below to see the gifts you get.**

YES! I have scratched off the silver box. Please send me all the gifts for which I qualify. I understand I am under no obligation to purchase any books, as explained on the back and on the opposite page.

106 CIH CCNH
(U-H-P-10/97)

NAME

ADDRESS   APT.

CITY   STATE   ZIP

 WORTH FOUR FREE BOOKS AND A SURPRISE MYSTERY GIFT!

 WORTH THREE FREE BOOKS

 **WORTH TWO FREE BOOKS**

 WORTH ONE FREE BOOK

Offer limited to one per household and not valid to current Harlequin Presents® subscribers. All orders subject to approval.

© 1990 HARLEQUIN ENTERPRISES LIMITED   **PRINTED IN U.S.A.**

DETACH AND MAIL CARD TODAY

THE HARLEQUIN READER SERVICE®: HERE'S HOW IT WORKS

Accepting free books places you under no obligation to buy anything. You may keep the books and gift and return the shipping statement marked "cancel". If you do not cancel, about a month later we'll send you 6 additional novels, and bill you just $2.90 each plus 25¢ delivery per book and applicable sales tax, if any.* That's the complete price–and compared to cover prices of $3.50 each–quite a bargain! You may cancel at any time, but if you choose to continue, every month we'll send you 6 more books, which you may either purchase at the discount price…or return to us and cancel your subscription.

*Terms and prices subject to change without notice. Sales tax applicable in N.Y.

'Fifteen minutes, you said?' She spoke to the Contessa. 'Do you mind if I use the telephone? I have a couple of calls I need to make.'

The Contessa agreed; she hadn't much choice.

Marlene almost laughed when she saw the questioning looks that flashed between the three of them. Let them wonder. Her business was her own affair, and, with an admonishment to Paul to be good, she walked back into the house. At last the gloves were coming off, Marlene thought, and perhaps this whole mess could be sorted out painlessly and quickly for all parties.

She had already decided there was no way she was hanging around just so Paul could keep the villa. The thought of following the boy around this place every summer for the next five years, simply to make sure he did not plunge down the steps, the cliffs, or drown in the pool, sounded like the holiday from hell! She didn't even like the villa, and they didn't need the money. No, she would keep faith with his father by bringing Paul on holiday every year. She would let him get to know the country and the people, but from the comfort of a hotel in Naples. According to Paolo, he had spent most of his time living in the penthouse on top of the Rossi building in that city.

Ten minutes later Marlene replaced the telephone in its cradle, a puzzled frown creasing her smooth brow. She could hear the high-pitched laughter of Paul in the distance and the deeper tone of Rocco's laughter, and for a second she wished she could join them—a bit of light-hearted fun would go down well right now. The news she had just received from her investigative friend in London was so odd it was amazing! It made no sense at all. Still frowning, she made her way to the study.

The Contessa was sitting in a high-backed chair behind a large black desk. Whoever designed this place must have had a passion for black! The inconsequential thought fluttered in Marlene's mind, and then she noticed that Andretti senior was standing at the Contessa's side.

Two against one was hardly fair, but Marlene said nothing; she simply sat down in the black leather chair the Contessa indicated.

'Miss Johanson, you must realise this is a very delicate situation,' Signor Andretti began, in slow but good English. 'As my son told you, my firm is dealing with the late Signor Rossi's estate. As you also know, this house is bequeathed to your half-brother on certain conditions. I must declare my interest here. I did not agree with Rossi leaving the boy this property on any condition, and if you will allow me I will explain why.'

'Yes, please go on,' she responded coolly, while wondering sadly if Paolo had ever realised before he died just how disloyal his friend and lawyer really was.

'I can see you are a sensible lady,' he said ingratiatingly, before continuing, 'I dislike speaking ill of the dead, but I feel Rossi left the villa to the boy simply out of spite.'

Marlene stiffened in her chair. The Paolo Rossi she had known had not had a spiteful bone in his body. 'I don't—'

'No, please allow me to finish. The original house on this site was a small, shabby affair—nothing like the beautiful building you see now. And it is all the Contessa's doing. It was designed and built to the Contessa's specifications. It was her creation, if you like, ten years ago, and she is very reluctant to part with it, as you can imagine. Her late husband admittedly owned it, and paid for the complete rebuilding, but he never appreciated the style and only ever visited the new villa once.'

Somehow Marlene was not surprised. The house suited the Contessa; it was as sharp and sterile as the woman herself appeared to be, and in a way it was a relief to know that her beloved Paolo had never considered the place his home.

'He altered his will some three and a half years ago, bequeathing the villa to the boy simply, I am sorry to say, because the Contessa—quite rightly, as a good Catholic—refused to give him the divorce he wanted. Now we are hoping you will be reasonable. The Contessa loves this place and is prepared to pay you a considerable amount of money to retain her sole ownership of the property.'

'How very generous,' Marlene drawled, the sarcasm lost on the other two.

'Yes, we are prepared to be so.' Andretti mentioned a figure that Marlene knew was ridiculously cheap for a prime piece of real estate in a prestigious area like Amalfi. 'And of course the Contessa will not insist that the boy comply with the conditions of the will before handing over the money. It can be arranged in a couple of days, and then you and the boy have no need to stay two months this year or any other year.'

'But I did promise Paul a holiday,' Marlene objected, simply to make the man squirm. 'He will be very disappointed.'

'No, no...you misunderstand. Now you are here, obviously you must enjoy your holiday. That goes without saying,' the older Andretti shot back placatingly.

As it happened, Marlene wasn't bothered on either count—the money or the holiday. She had already made her decision, but she was not about to tell them that. Instead she spent an eventful half-hour haggling up the price, and then, with handshakes all round, it was agreed. As compensation it was a derisory amount, given the value of the property, and the avarice she could see in their eyes said as much, but Marlene pretended not to notice, nor to hear their brief exchange in Italian.

'I told you, Carlo, she is a fool—she knows nothing. I don't know why your son could not have settled this business last week—the shares, the villa, everything— and then the woman need never have come here.'

'You're right—typical of him. He is probably more interested in getting the woman into his bed than in business.'

Marlene hid her smile behind a pretend yawn. The father surely knew his son, and obviously did not think much of his legal skills. 'If you don't mind,' she interrupted, rising to her feet, 'I find all this business talk tiring. I could use a cup of coffee.'

'There is one other little matter I would like to discuss with you,' the senior Andretti said quickly. 'Your shares in the company.'

'Oh, please can we discuss that another time? Today is Sunday—a day of rest. I imagine it will take a few days for all the legal documents to be organised, and, as I said, I did promise Paul a holiday. So, if it is all right with you, Contessa, we will leave next Saturday.'

Surprise fought with triumph on the Contessa's fine features. She had obviously not hoped to be rid of her so quickly.

'But of course, Miss Johanson. Enjoy your week.' The woman agreed so speedily it was almost insulting. 'Unfortunately we have to return to Naples today, but Signor Andretti will return later in the week and conclude our business, *sì*?'

Marlene almost said no, but she saw no reason to enlighten the woman after the information she had received this morning. The board meeting was on Friday; the timing was perfect for Marlene. She could stir up a hornet's nest and walk away the next day. She might not save Paolo Rossi's name, but she fully intended to expose the people who had betrayed him. 'I will look forward to his visit,' she replied noncommittally.

'Good. Now enjoy the weather. I will send Eta out to the patio with coffee.'

As a dismissal it was classic, Marlene thought, but with a bland smile she said, 'Thank you.'

It was a relief to get back out into the fresh air. Paul and Rocco were nowhere in sight, and she did not feel like looking for them. She needed time to assimilate all she had learned from her telephone conversation, and form a plan of campaign. She sat down on an intricately wrought iron chair, one of six around the large oval matching table. Yet more glass, she mused as Eta appeared with a tray holding a coffee-pot, cup and saucer, milk and sugar.

'*Grazie, Eta,*' she said with a smile and, lifting the pot, she filled the cup with the rich aromatic brew. She stirred in a little sugar, and was just raising the cup to her lips when Paul suddenly appeared at the top of the steps from the lower terrace.

Marlene took a drink of the hot liquid and set the cup back on the table, flashing the boy a broad smile. 'Having fun?' she called.

He raced across to her side. 'Mar, Roc took me right down to the bottom of the cliff.'

'What? Wasn't that dangerous?' Marlene asked anxiously. It looked impossible from where she was sitting.

'No, it wasn't,' Rocco answered, crossing the terrace in a few lithe strides to stand towering over her.

She tilted her head back to look up at him, shading her eyes from the sun with her hand. 'So you say,' she said curtly. She had not forgotten Caterina's comment when they had first arrived, about getting rid of the pair of them.

'You are doubting my word? You seriously think I would put the boy's life in danger?' Rocco demanded, sliding into the chair opposite her, the brief smile curling his sensuous lips belied by the hard gleam in his black eyes.

She eyed him dispassionately. Rocco was wearing plain white shorts and a white sleeveless sweatshirt, and the overall effect of his midnight-black hair and deeply tanned skin against the white was stunning. But then he would be a striking male in any company; he had an intrinsic aura of danger about him that even his seemingly relaxed position—one foot casually lifted across one knee—did nothing to dispel. She shivered for no apparent reason.

'Well? Do you?' he demanded, stony-faced.

She met his eyes levelly. 'I really don't know. I don't know you.' Marlene doubted he would harm a child, but she refused to back down beneath his quelling gaze. 'I don't know how far you would go to protect those you consider your friends, like Caterina and the Contessa.'

'My God, you have some opinion of me.' Rocco sat up in the chair and, leaning across the table, explained tautly, 'I carried Paul down the steps that are cut into the cliff to the sea. *Carried* him! Understand? He was never in any danger. I showed him where his father used to take me as a young boy, where he taught me to fish, before he was even married to the Contessa. I thought it might help Paul to know something of his family history.

'The Rossis were the...what is the word?' He frowned. 'The blacksmiths in Amalfi for generations. Originally Paul's grandfather built a house here in the thirties. He was a shrewd man. He could see even then that the area was becoming a haunt of the rich and famous. He rented it out to supplement his income and then Paolo Rossi lived here when he first started his engineering business. My mother owned the next house around the cliff. Rossi and my parents were good friends until—'

'I got a piggy-back, Mar—all the way down and all the way up.' Paul chose that moment to butt in.

Until what? she wondered, fascinated by the brief glimpse of the past. But she did not ask; instead, dragging her eyes away from the furious glitter in Rocco's, she turned to Paul. 'That's lovely, darling, but don't ever try to go down the steps yourself. Promise?'

'I already promised Roc. Not ever.' He shook his little head to emphasise the point.

'Satisfied?' Rocco drawled sardonically.

'I suppose I will have to be,' she said with bad grace, and was saved from having to say anything further when Eta appeared.

She pretended not to listen as Rocco asked for another cup and an orange juice for the boy. Instead she picked up her own cup and sipped the coffee. But when he turned his attention to Paul she stiffened defensively.

'Go along with Eta, Paul. You can bring my cup back after you have had your orange juice.'

The last thing she needed was to be left alone with Rocco, even for a minute. 'He doesn't—' she began, but Rocco cut her off.

'Run along, Paul. I will keep Mar company until you get back.' And, with a gentle pat on the little boy's bottom, he sent him on his way.

Marlene watched the departing duo with dismay. She wasn't fooled for a second. Rocco's use of 'Mar' had been quite deliberate. He had not forgotten last night— nor forgiven, by the sound of it.

'So, Marlene...' His dark brows lifted ironically. 'Alone at last! Afraid?'

'Why on earth should I be?' she said, with a careless shrug of her shoulders. 'Paul will be back in a minute.' Marlene made herself look into his dark eyes. 'I can't see you seducing me in front of a little boy, Rocco.' She smiled—a slow curl of her full lips. 'However much you may want to.' She knew damn fine that seduction was not what he had in mind, but she wasn't going to give him the chance to vent his anger on her. Not if she could help it.

'You don't fool me for a moment, Marlene.' He reached across the table and caught her hand in his. 'If I wanted to, I could seduce you in thirty seconds flat, and you know it.' And, rubbing his thumb across her palm, he moved his fingers to her wrist.

'Let go of me.' She tried to pull her hand free. The warmth of his touch brought an immediate response to her body that she could not control, and she knew he was well aware of the fact.

'No, I like to feel your pulse flutter beneath my fingers.' Rocco laughed under his breath at her gasp of outrage. 'You shouldn't dish it out if you can't take it, Marlene.'

She threw him an angry glance. 'I won't argue with you. There's no point.'

His slow smile was chilling as his fingers tightened around her wrist. 'I'm glad you realise that, Marlene, because I want some straight answers from you and I intend to have them. This afternoon after lunch Paul will take a nap, and then you and I will talk.' His voice was as cold as his smile.

He watched her intently, the silence stretching as she sought for some response. Then Paul's little voice could be heard, yelling that he was on his way, and Marlene heaved a sigh of relief.

Rocco let go of her hand. 'Don't make me come looking for you, lady, or you will regret it,' he grated softly just as Paul arrived at his side with a cup in his hand.

Once more in her bedroom, Marlene divested Paul of his clothes and watched as he pulled on his still damp swimming trunks. Then she went into the bathroom and quickly slipped out of her clothes and back into her swimsuit. It was barely eleven o'clock, she realised, walking back into the room, and this was the third time they had dressed and undressed. A deep sigh escaped her. It was turning into a hell of a morning!

'Right, pet, back to the pool—but first some sun cream.' When she was satisfied that they were both adequately protected against the fierce rays of the summer sun, she slung a towel around her shoulders, caught Paul's hand in hers and set off for the swimming pool yet again.

Marlene hesitated before stepping outside. Rocco, his father, the Contessa and Caterina were all standing in a group, apparently arguing. Suddenly she saw Rocco gesticulate wildly, and heard his deep voice declaring angrily in Italian, 'I can understand the Contessa's point of view, though I don't agree with it—she was a deserted wife. But *you*, Papà, for God's sake! Whatever the woman was or was not the boy is innocent, and you are deliberately robbing Rossi's son of his inheritance. This place is worth ten times that and you know it.'

'It doesn't concern you any more. I ask you once in your life to make a simple deal, and you can't do it. You would never make a lawyer in a hundred years. You always were far too much like your mother—taking the moral high ground. Well, forget it. It is settled, and we are leaving now.'

What might have followed Marlene would never know, because at that moment Paul decided he had hung around long enough, and said in a high-pitched treble, 'Come on, Mar, hurry up.'

As she walked out onto the terrace all eyes turned to her, the sudden silence making it embarrassingly obvious that they had been talking about her.

'Miss Johanson.' The Contessa was the first to recover. 'I was just asking Rocco where you were. I am sorry, we must leave now.'

Marlene watched as the little woman walked towards her. Today the Contessa was dressed in a red, white and black tunic in a dramatic design, and white silk trousers, and her face was half-hidden by a large floppy-brimmed red hat. She held out a bejewelled hand to Marlene. '*Arrivederci*. I doubt we will meet again. But as we agreed Signor Andretti will finish the business, no?'

'Of course,' Marlene agreed. But not in the way this woman imagined, she thought secretly. She shook hands with the Contessa, and then, after perfunctory farewells from Caterina and Carlo Andretti, two minutes later there was only Rocco, Paul and a very puzzled Marlene left.

Through her bewilderment she managed to retain enough control to be wryly amused at the mass exodus. The bimbo had been conned and they were gone. But that did not explain Rocco's attitude. He had actually been defending Paul, and indirectly her... Nor did it explain why he was still here. Unless he still meant to have the conversation with her which he had threatened earlier...

'We're going for a swim.' She stated the obvious, unsettled by this different view of Rocco, and also filled with sympathy for the man. His father's slating of his legal abilities had been cruel, and somehow hadn't rung true. He had an aura of power, a confidence about him that was undeniable. Or was that just her reaction to him? she asked herself, and shivered. 'When are you leaving?' she asked suddenly, as it hit her that in a few short days she would be going back to England and would never see this man again.

He simply stared at her, and there was such open desire in the unsmiling look he gave her that her nipples hardened beneath the damp fabric of her bathing suit. She shivered again, suddenly overwhelmed by the intensity of her reactions. She gripped Paul's hand tighter, the silence getting to her. 'Would you like to come swimming with us?' she blurted—anything to break the tension.

'Yes,' Rocco said, his eyes never leaving her. 'I'll go and change.' But he didn't move. She had no idea how stunning she looked. Her lovely face was devoid of make-up, her long blonde hair was tied back in a ponytail, and her skin, tanned a light gold, contrasted with the plain white bathing suit. The damp suit was high-cut, exaggerating her long legs and outlining her feminine curves in intimate detail.

'Well...' she murmured, her colour high. 'See you.' And, with Paul tugging at her hand, she sidestepped around Rocco. She felt his eyes burning into her back as she walked across to the pool.

Marlene jumped into the welcoming water and, turning, held out her arms for Paul. In her peripheral vision she saw Rocco turn and enter the house. What on earth had possessed her to ask him to join them? She knew he was furious with her. She must be mad.

And five minutes later she knew she was, when Rocco appeared at the edge of the pool. For a heart-stopping moment she thought he was naked...

CHAPTER SEVEN

ROCCO was standing balancing on the balls of his feet, just about to dive in. His body was deeply tanned and supple, his muscular chest covered with a light brushing of black hair, arrowing down his belly. He was wearing a very brief pair of tan swimming trunks that cupped his manhood and nothing much else. The colour blended so closely with his skin tone that at first she really had thought he was naked.

He grinned as he saw her glancing at them. 'For Paul's sake. Normally I don't bother when I'm alone, or with a beautiful woman. Disappointed?'

Disappointed! Marlene seriously doubted there was a woman in the world who would find Rocco disappointing, even if he was dressed in rags. He was a superb specimen of the male sex, and he knew it. To hide her embarrassment at being caught staring at him, she swam across the pool to where Paul was gamely swimming along—but within reach of the side, as she had told him.

'Coward!' Rocco cried, before executing a perfect dive and entering the water with hardly a splash.

Surprisingly, the next half-hour was pure fun. Rocco surfaced right beside Paul and proceeded to play with the boy in the water. A ball was found and Marlene was roped into a hilarious game of piggy-in-the-middle—and of course the two males made her the piggy first. She didn't mind; she was simply relieved that Rocco appeared to have forgotten his anger and dire threats of earlier.

Paul was too small to play in the water, so he took up position on the side of the pool, with Marlene swimming around a few feet away and Rocco behind her. It was exhausting but exhilarating. Rocco seemed to take a perverse delight in jumping almost on top of her, never mind where the ball was. Paul roared with laughter in between yelling, 'Get Mar—get her!'

So much for family loyalty, Marlene thought, swimming rapidly to where the ball had landed in the deepest part of the pool. She closed her arms around it, and in her excitement at finally winning shouted, '*Vincita*—I win!' Only to have two strong hands close around her slender waist and drag her down beneath the water. She lost the ball, but that was the least of her worries.

In a tangle of arms and legs they sank to the bottom of the pool. Rocco's strongly muscled thigh slid between her wildly kicking legs and pressed against the most intimate part of her body. Holding her down with one arm anchored around her waist, he slid his hand up over her breast, lingering until he felt her nipple peak in stark arousal, before curving it up and around her throat.

His hard mouth covered hers. She grasped his shoulders, his neck—anywhere—and hung on, the feel of his near-naked body hard against her sending shock waves of sensual awareness surging through her. Eyes tightly closed, she opened her mouth to the pressure of his, and their tongues met and stroked and sucked. Her hand slid over his shoulder and traced his spine as she had imagined doing earlier. She was drowning in a sea of sensations she had never suspected existed before.

They almost did drown, as neither could bear to break the passionate embrace. Finally they rose to the surface, both breathless. Their eyes locked, Rocco's black with passion and Marlene's wide, golden and dazzled by the man whose strong arm was still curved around her waist. She needed the support. Her insides had turned to jelly and her flesh burned with a fire the cool water could not assuage.

For a long piquant moment they simply stared at each other, both of one mind. The mutual need, want, had been recognised and finally accepted between them.

'You kissed my Mar,' was the first thing Marlene registered over the pounding of her heart.

She tore her gaze away from Rocco at the same time as she pushed out of his arms, and, not daring to look at him, she swam to the side and dragged herself out of the water.

Rocco was right behind her, but he did not get out of the pool. Instead, he clung to the side and, grinning up at Paul's serious face, said, 'Yes, I kissed Marlene—and very nice it was too.'

Marlene was flushed from head to toe with embarrassment and the lingering effects of her passionate encounter with Rocco. 'Really, Rocco,' she remonstrated. 'Paul is too young for that kind of talk.'

'Don't be such a prude. He is half-Italian, after all, and Italian boys understand the delightful difference between the male and the female much sooner than most.'

If it was possible, Marlene's face turned even redder. He was deliberately teasing her, she knew, but she wasn't going to let him get away with it. 'Come out of the pool and say that,' she charged, and, arching one delicately shaped brow, added slyly, 'If you dare.' She had a good idea why he was hiding in the water. Her flesh was still tingling from the pressure of his rock-hard arousal and, remembering the brevity of his swimming trunks, she doubted he was in a fit state to reveal himself.

'Dare? I dare anything. But are you sure you're ready for this, Marlene?' And, laughing at her shocked expression, he leant his arms on the side of the pool and was halfway out of the water in a second.

'No!' she cried, and, catching him off guard, she lashed out with one slender foot at his broad shoulder and pushed. He fell backwards into the water with a great splash, his arms splaying in the air as his head sank below the surface. Strike one for me, she thought smugly.

'Come on, Paul.' Taking her brother's hand, she pulled him away from the poolside and headed towards the house. 'We've both had enough of the sun for one day— we don't want to burn.' The trouble was, she thought with fatalistic conviction, it was too late for her. She would burn for Rocco for the rest of her life.

'But what about Roc?' Paul demanded.

'He's big enough to look after himself,' she muttered, and then, glancing back over her shoulder, she stopped, her temperature soaring again as Rocco hauled himself out of the pool in one lithe movement. With the water running off his splendid torso, his black hair plastered to his head and chest, he took her breath away. He looked like some mythical Greek god rising from the deep. He straightened up and his eyes caught her glance. She expected him to be furious but he confounded her. Shaking his head in a shower of waterdrops glistening in the noon sun like a halo, he strode towards her.

'Marlene, you're a constant source of surprise, with the depths of hidden secrets in your golden eyes which a man could spend a lifetime trying to unravel,' Rocco told her with a wry grin.

'I don't know what you mean,' she said haughtily.

Rocco chuckled, and, throwing an arm around her shoulders, he commanded, 'Come on, let's go inside and cool off.' Catching Paul with his free hand, he swung him up in his other arm. 'Your sister is feeling the heat, Paul, and we men have to look after the ladies,' he opined, with a wickedly sexual slanting glance at Marlene's scarlet face.

She would never understand Rocco in a million years, Marlene thought a little while later. The three of them were sitting around the stainless-steel table in the kitchen, still in their swimwear, and tucking into a lunch of various cold meats along with several types of salad and

an assortment of fresh fruit. When Marlene had suggested they should get changed before lunch, Rocco had
quickly declared that it was not necessary and had gone
on to explain that Eta and Aldo usually had Sunday off.
They had only stayed this morning because of Marlene's
visit. Now they had left and would not be back until
tomorrow morning. They had the place to themselves
and casual was the order of the day.

She wasn't sure she liked the idea of being in the house
with only Rocco and Paul for company. But as they
hungrily devoured the food Rocco, with his easy humour
and casual conversation and almost brotherly behaviour
towards herself and Paul, lulled her into a sense of se-
curity. He really was a very nice man...

Marlene drained her glass of mineral water and after
replacing it on the table sat back with a sigh of con-
tentment. She didn't know why Rocco's attitude had
changed so drastically from the brooding, angry man of
this morning, but she was too happy to query it. For a
while at least she was determined to forget why she was
here and simply enjoy the moment.

'Had enough to eat, Paul?' she asked, smiling as he
tried to stuff one more juicy strawberry in his mouth,
almost missing and smearing his nose with red juice.

'Yes,' he said, and, yawning widely, added, 'I'm full.'

'You're also tired,' Rocco said softly, and, getting to
his feet, he picked Paul out of his chair and swung him
up in his arms. 'Time for a nap, little man.'

Marlene expected her brother to protest, but to her
amazement he laid his head on Rocco's broad shoulder
and mumbled, 'Yes.'

They made a lovely picture—the boy's dark head
cradled close to the man's equally dark one by a strong,
protective hand. They could almost be father and son,
she thought, and the idea brought a dreamy glow to
Marlene's eyes. To have Rocco's baby, to have him hold

her in the same protective way as he held Paul would be heaven...

'I hope you're not falling asleep on me as well.' Rocco's husky drawl snapped her out of her daydream and, flushing scarlet, she jumped out of her seat.

'No, no, of course not. Give him to me.' She faced him with her head high and her back straight. Her dishevelled blonde hair was almost dry now, and beginning to curl haphazardly around her shoulders. 'I'll put him to bed.' And she held out her arms expectantly.

His eyes held hers for a moment, and then they dropped, travelling over her, insolently lingering where her swimsuit moulded to her breasts and hips. A mocking smile curved his lips. 'No, I will. I think you'd better get some clothes on—unless you want me to put you to bed as well.'

Marlene bristled like an angry cat. 'In your dreams,' she snapped.

'You're already in my dreams,' he said throatily. 'And if I wasn't carrying Paul I'd give you a taste of the reality.' A gleam of sensual amusement made his dark eyes sparkle, and ignited an answering sparkle in Marlene's.

'You're impossible,' she opined, with a slight smile and a rueful shake of her fair head. She glanced at Paul; he was fast asleep in Rocco's arms. Now was no time to argue, and, turning, she said, 'Follow me.'

She walked straight through her bedroom and into the dressing room. She picked up the coverlet from the narrow bed and murmured softly, 'Be careful—lower him down gently and I'll tuck him in.'

'I'm not about to drop him from a great height,' Rocco drawled sarcastically, while placing Paul carefully on the bed.

'I know.' Marlene felt ashamed of herself. 'I didn't mean to imply you would,' she said, keeping her voice low.

'Good.' Rocco straightened up and inadvertently brushed against her shoulder. He put out a hand to steady her, and the light touch was enough to make her tense.

She glanced up at him. Their eyes met and held and Marlene felt her heart begin to beat faster. She dropped her head and bent over the bed. Fussily she set about arranging the cover over the sleeping child—anything to avoid looking at the man beside her.

'Relax, Marlene, I'm going for a shower and to change. I suggest you do the same.' And with a last look at the sleeping boy Rocco walked out of the room.

Marlene tossed her head back and let the powerful spray wash the last of the shampoo out of her long hair, then, turning off the shower, she stepped out of the cubicle and picked a fluffy white towel off the black towel rail. She wrapped it around her naked body, tying it in a knot between her breasts. Taking another, smaller towel, she briskly rubbed the excess water from her hair and crossed the vanity basin. A hairdryer was conveniently attached to the wall, and with little effort she turned it on and began the tedious process of drying her hair.

Gradually her mind went back over the events of the past two days as mechanically she brushed and blow-dried her hair. Rocco's meeting her at the airport had been a shock, but she could not deny that her heart had skipped a beat, and the instant attraction she had felt for him the first time she had seen him had been as strong as ever, if not more so... But the fact that he worked for the Contessa—even if he had appeared to defend Paul over the sale of the house this morning—meant that though she might love him she could never trust him. Her hand stopped in mid-sweep, and she stared at her reflection in the vanity mirror. The dreamy-eyed image that stared back at her horrified her.

Love! Oh, no! She couldn't! She must not love the man. Physical attraction, lust—anything but love. She brushed her hair with renewed vigour, trying to blot out her wayward thoughts with the sound of the dryer. Think of the information from the telephone call this morning, she told herself firmly, which virtually confirms Andretti's deceit. But somehow all she could think about was being in Rocco's arms.

She remembered the first evening he had taken her out to dinner, how she had returned to her own home and melted into his arms in her own hallway. She had almost let him make love to her! It was no wonder he had believed she had been an old man's mistress—a woman who made love easily and freely. She had behaved no better today, entwined in his embrace in the swimming pool. It was an intolerable situation. She had to keep him at arm's length for the next few days—at least until the board meeting was over.

A small voice whispered derisively in her head, Who are you kidding? He touches you and you melt. Marlene wanted to deny it, but her own innate honesty would not let her. She sighed and, tilting her head to the side, flicked the hairdryer under her hair one last time. Then, straightening up, she reached to switch it off. But another hand was there before her.

'What...' The word echoed in the sudden silence. She half turned, and Rocco was standing right beside her. The sound of the hairdryer had masked his entry.

His hand slid into her hair and he stroked its length. 'It's beautiful, like spun gold,' he said huskily, his dark eyes fixed on her shining hair.

Marlene trembled. She was standing naked but for a towel, and Rocco was far too close and far too tempting. He had changed into shorts and a short-sleeved shirt he had not bothered to fasten. 'Wh-what are you doing?' she stammered inanely.

His hand tangled in her hair and he tugged, pulling back her head. 'I'm kissing you,' he said, and his mouth slowly lowered to her lips, as if he was giving her time to object.

She knew she should reject him, escape, but her foolish heart would not let her. She felt his muscular arm enfold her and draw her close even as his mouth touched hers, warm and strangely tender, as if he was reassuring her, dispelling all her fears. All thought of resistance vanished. She met his kiss with her own, mouth soft and lips gently parted, and when his tongue probed the warm, moist depths a shudder of desire arched through her body.

His hand tightened in her hair and then loosened, his fingers drifting to where the towel was secured between her breasts. His thumb brushed enticingly across a hard peak, and then with one swift movement the towel fell apart.

Marlene made a little cry of protest which died when his other hand stroked down over her bottom and the towel fell to the floor. His mouth lifted from hers and he looked down into her golden eyes, then lower, to where the fullness of her breasts was exposed to his hungry gaze, and lower still, to where golden curls marked the centre of her femininity. Cool air touched her and with it doubt. But even as she thought of resistance he groaned—a harsh, guttural sound.

'God, but you're magnificent,' he grated as he bent her over one arm. His dark head lowered and his tongue rasped across one aching breast; with his other hand he cupped its partner and teased the sensitive peak between his fingers. As his mouth suckled her she knew she was powerless to deny him, or herself...

Her hand came up and clasped his head, holding him to her breast, inviting him, urging him to continue. His fingers teased and tortured, and heat and hunger for him welled up inside her like a tidal wave. She gasped and clung to him when he lifted his head and drew away slightly. She stared up at him and saw the stark, glittering desire glowing in his eyes. He wanted her as desperately as she wanted him.

'Rocco.' She whispered his name and then his mouth covered hers again, and she was lost in a sensual world of feeling where only his touch existed. She slid her hands down over his hair-roughened chest and up and under his shirt, her hands stroking up his bare back.

'Yes, yes,' Rocco growled, and, swinging her into his arms, one arm beneath her knees and the other around her back, he carried her into the bedroom.

'Paul—we can't—' She tried to object but he simply lifted her higher, his hair brushing her burning skin as he buried his head between her naked breasts, kissing the silken hollow before letting his tongue flick each taut nipple in turn. And she was lost once more—lost in realms of sensual pleasure she had never dreamed possible.

'We can.' He spoke against her flesh. 'Trust me.'

He lowered her onto the bed, and her eyes flew open when he left her. She had just begun to focus enough to realise that she was stark naked in a room she had never seen before, and to wonder how on earth she had let it go so far, when her gaze fell on Rocco and she had her answer. He had thrown off his shirt and was unfastening the snap of his shorts. Mesmerised, she watched as he removed a packet from his pocket, dropped it on the bedside table, then stripped off his shorts and briefs in one fluid movement before turning to her.

Her gasp of awe was tinged with a feminine fear. He was unashamedly, magnificently male, his bronzed body gleaming in a ray of sunlight streaming through the window.

Then he was beside her, and he breathed her name in a low, throaty growl. 'Marlene—at last. Let me look at you.' And, propping his head on his arm, he stared down at her softly shaped feminine form with rapt attention. He trailed one finger from her mouth to her chin, down her throat, over the valley of her breast, across her navel and to the tangle of curls at the juncture of her thighs.

'Rocco, it's daylight,' she groaned suddenly, overcome with embarrassment even as her flesh quivered in ecstasy at his touch. 'We should talk...' She was babbling, but the enormity of what she was about to do had finally sunk into her bemused brain. She had only ever had one lover—Julian—and it had not been much fun. She had not really enjoyed it.

Rocco, his black eyes burning into hers, rasped, 'Later, my lovely little liar. I have to have you now.' And he blocked any response by kissing her, his mouth hard and demanding, branding her his.

A brief warning flashed in her mind. 'Lovely little liar'—he had not forgotten. Fighting her arousal, she tried to say no. But as his long fingers delved into the soft curls to the hot, moist warmth beneath she betrayed herself and moaned, 'Yes,' her legs parting involuntarily as he stoked the fire of her sexuality with teasing touches and silken caresses. Marlene let her love and her need for him sweep away all her reservations and inhibitions, glorying in his masculinity.

Her small hands curved up over his broad chest. She scratched a small male nipple and felt him tremble. Then her hands curved round his back, her nails digging into his flesh as the tension inside her built to fever-pitch. She stroked one hand down over his hard buttock and round to his flat stomach, loving the feel of his satin-smooth flesh beneath her fingers, the pulsating power of his manhood.

It was Rocco's turn to groan. 'Yes. God, yes!' And, reaching to the bedside table, he quickly found the protection.

Before Marlene had time to realise what he was doing he was kneeling between her thighs, his hands curved under her bottom. He lifted her up to him and then he kissed her. Her head fell back and her heart seemed to stop. Never had she been kissed so intimately. She tried again to say no, but it was lost; she could not deny her innermost desire as he moved swiftly over and into her. She winced once, and he stopped.

'You're not a virgin?' he groaned, his muscles bunching as he fought for control, his tormented black eyes burning down into hers.

But her body was adapting to his size and power and she clenched around him. 'No—no!' she cried, desperate for him to continue. 'It's been a long—' She didn't finish. Rocco thrust again and their bodies fused in a fierce, primitive rhythm.

The passion that exploded between them was ferocious and total. The climax, when it came, was so savage and so exquisitely prolonged that Marlene realised in a moment of blinding clarity that this was the man she had been born for. Her past experience was as nothing to the wonder of Rocco. She lay entangled with him as passion gave way to languor, relishing their closeness as she held his hot, sweat-soaked body against her, and as he moved her arms tightened around his back, reluctant to let him go.

'I'm too heavy,' he gasped raggedly, fighting to steady his breathing.

'No,' she murmured, looking up into his dark face, 'you're perfect.'

He smiled and gently brushed her swollen lips with his. 'No, darling,' he said, and, easing onto his side, he leant over her, carefully sweeping a few strands of blonde hair from her damp brow. '*You're* perfect.'

Her golden eyes gleamed up into his. 'Are we going to argue again?' she teased, lifting her hands to rest on his broad chest, loving this tender side of him.

He caught her hands in one of his, and slid his other arm under her shoulders, holding her close to him. 'We are never going to argue again,' Rocco declared emphatically. 'What we have together is too magnificent...too...' He squeezed her hands against his chest, his dark eyes searching her lovely face. 'I can't find the words in English to tell you how you make me feel.'

She gazed up at him, her golden eyes still glowing with the embers of passion. 'I know,' she said simply. An arrested expression flitted across his handsome face, and she wondered if he had realised she loved him. But she could not have been more wrong.

His shrewd dark eyes narrowed on her upturned face. 'You and I have to talk.'

'Must we?' Marlene murmured, running her foot lightly up his muscular leg, trying to divert him. For some reason he sounded grim, and it frightened her. She did not want to lose the elation, the intimate bonding their lovemaking had created—not yet! Not ever!

'Stop that.' His legs moved to trap hers and, freeing her hands, he lifted his hand to cup her chin. 'You cried out in the pool today in Italian, and I haven't forgotten how you pretended to be Rossi's mistress and Paul's mother.'

'Rocco, I... Paul will be awake...' She was searching for an excuse to delay the inevitable.

He stopped her words with a hard command. 'Whatever you are going to say, try making it the truth this time, Marlene.' His voice was flat, devoid of any emotion, and a chill shivered over her naked flesh.

She looked into his taut face and cold black eyes returned her gaze. Her teeth worried at her lip; she wasn't sure what to say, what to do. Surely he could not make love to her so desperately one minute and then reject her the next? Yet that was what it felt like. Maybe to him it was just sex... Shame and humiliation swept over her. She had given her heart and he had given nothing.

She closed her eyes, fighting back the tears, battling to regain her self-control. She refused to give him the satisfaction of knowing he had hurt her, and, adopting a mantle of cool reserve, she said simply, 'Let me up and I'll explain.'

'All right.' His voice was clipped. His hands and legs left her and he stood up.

She opened her eyes and, very aware of her naked state, sat up and pulled the coverlet up to her chin.

Rocco pulled on his shorts, sat down on the edge of the bed and said curtly, 'Begin.'

She searched his starkly austere face for some sign of the lover of moments ago, but it was a futile task. He had hooked one leg over his knee, his body angled towards her, and the light gleamed on his broad, tanned shoulders, outlining his handsome features. But she could see no expression in his partially hooded eyes. 'I don't know where to start,' she began, all her earlier reservations about Rocco suddenly returning to torment her.

'At the beginning is usually a good idea,' he said sardonically.

'Thank you,' she replied sarcastically, and, remembering the beginning, she went white to the lips. How could she have been so dumb? His plan had been to seduce her and he had certainly succeeded. With the realisation something snapped inside her. She sat up straighter, tucked the coverlet under her arms and let him have it...

'Paolo and my mother loved each other deeply—something you would not understand.' She fired the words at him, thinking bitterly of how very recently she had deluded herself in his arms. But she would not let herself think of her humiliation; she was too angry. 'You and Caterina appeared at my home, decided I was Rossi's mistress and roundly insulted me, my mother and Paul. And, yes, I *do* speak Italian—very well. As I recall, "low-life" was mentioned, "peasant" and "bastard", to name but a few.

'Then, of course, there was the plan to seduce me—the unfit mother scam to gain control of the boy.' Her eyes spitting fury as she warmed to her theme, she continued, 'Oh, and let's not forget Caterina's latest idea. You should have dropped us over a cliff on the way here. You make me sick. You have the audacity to question *me* about the truth? Don't make me laugh... Just get out!'

His face went grey beneath his tan. 'Oh, my God!' he breathed, and for a moment she thought she saw anguish in his dark eyes. But she was wrong. It was anger. With a terrific effort of will he suppressed the violent emotions her tirade had aroused and said coldly, 'But you know the old saying—eavesdroppers never hear good of themselves. I did ask if you spoke my language.'

'I see, so it's all my fault?' she spat.

'No, I am as much to blame. And I apologise if anything I said offended you. But I had seen you in a restaurant years earlier with Rossi—we were introduced. It was a natural mistake to make. A mistake, moreover, you could have corrected immediately with one word,' he drawled harshly.

'On that particular day Paolo and I had just come from the mortuary after identifying the mangled body of my mother. We couldn't have cared less what opinion you formed in your dirty mind. We had lost a woman we loved and had a one-year-old child to worry about. Whereas, if I recall correctly, your only problem was the red-haired woman hanging on your arm and a contemptuous holier-than-thou attitude. An attitude you still had when you appeared last week at The Johanson Herb Garden. Why the hell should I tell you anything?'

Rocco sucked in a deep breath, closed his eyes for a second and shivered. 'I did not know. I could not have known about your mother, and I'm sorry from the bottom of my heart.' And he looked at her with such compassion that Marlene almost believed him. Until he qualified his behaviour. 'I freely admit I should not have spoken to Caterina about you the way I did, but she is a friend of long standing and you I had only met once before. I was only trying to help her and her mother.'

'Help the Contessa to rob a young boy?' Marlene interjected.

'No, never that.'

'You're a lawyer—I thought they were supposed to have ethics? Though according to your father you're not a very good one,' she sneered.

A grim smile curved his hard mouth and, leaning forward on the bed, he grabbed her by the shoulders. His dark face was only inches from her own. 'I am not a lawyer. I was simply doing a favour for my father by accompanying Caterina to England and repeating what he had told me to say.'

'But you said—' she began angrily, then she stopped, confusion clearly visible in the golden eyes that met his gaze. Had he actually told her he was a lawyer? Or had he just said he was representing his father's firm?

His long fingers dug into her shoulders. 'Marlene, I think it is time for me to explain, before the confusion gets any worse. I am a consultant geologist for a host of large companies worldwide. I spend most of my time abroad—South America, Australia, Africa, wherever I am needed. I have a house not far from here, as I told you—my mother left it to me. It is my home, and I also have an office in Rome. My father has his law practice in Naples and an apartment there. We rarely see each other. As you have probably noticed, we do not get on very well together.'

'Why not?' The question slipped out. Her anger was fading in the face of his revelation. She was intrigued. She could see him as a geologist much more easily than as a lawyer. Now she understood the Contessa's comment about Rocco with his head in the ground and her lips twitched in amusement.

His hands loosened on her shoulders, stroking gently. 'It isn't funny. I was ten when I first discovered my father had a mistress and I saw my mother in tears. My mother should have left him then; she was a wealthy woman in her own right, half-Italian and half-Irish. Her father owned a large brewing company and a vineyard, and she was his sole heir. But it would not have suited my father; he liked having a string of mistresses,' Rocco said with a tinge of contempt.

'As a young man I had very little respect for my father, and the fact that I would not follow him into the law put a bigger strain on our relationship. A week after the death of my mother I went to South Africa, and when I returned to Italy, a couple of weeks ago, I suppose I thought I should try one last time to get on with my father. He is the only relative I have left. When he asked me to go to England and sort out the money-grubbing mistress Paolo Rossi had left behind, for the sake of the Contessa and Caterina I agreed.

'Our families have been friends for years, both spending the holidays here in Amalfi. I've got to know Caterina well—I think of her almost as a sister—and I learnt long ago the only way to handle her is to humour her. As a small child she would fly into a tantrum to get her own way, and though I have not seen as much of her over the past fifteen years it seems old habits die hard. An argument with Caterina is a futile exercise; it is much easier to agree with her even if one does not. But believe me,' he added darkly, 'no one regrets what was said more than me.

'I can't entirely blame Caterina; I was quite happy to go along with her. I have no excuse. I listened to my father's side of the story, damning the English mistress, and believed him. Perhaps I wanted to believe him because I had never quite been able to put your face out of my mind from that very first time I saw you in the restaurant with Paolo. I spoke to you and you barely registered I was there. I suppose my male ego took a blow... I thought, How could such a beautiful young girl possibly prefer an old man? Then, when I saw you again, the same thought taunted me and I wanted to believe the worst.

'I should have remembered there are always two sides in any broken relationship. I had no right to judge why Rossi parted from his wife or his choice of mistress. I wish I could take back the hard words I said about you and yours, but I can't. I formed a judgement on prejudice and my own wounded pride. I had no right. I can only say I am sorry. I hope you will forgive me.'

His apology sounded as sincere as it had been revealing, and Marlene would have liked to be able to accept it wholeheartedly and apologise honestly in return. But unfortunately she could not...

Picking her words carefully, she said in a voice tinged with regret for what might have been, 'We have both been playing games.' But a relationship without trust was a non-starter—even with her limited experience she knew that much—and even now she could not tell him the complete truth. 'I'm sorry for pretending to be Paolo's mistress and Paul's mother, and for not admitting I speak Italian. But my business will be settled and I will be out of here by next weekend. Perhaps we should just leave it at that.'

'I can't.' Rocco gave a small, ironic smile. 'Nor, I think, can you.'

'What do you mean?' A glimmer of hope leapt in her breast. Did he mean he cared enough to forget all the past mistakes?

'I behaved like a swine in England, and I'm sorry. But this thing between us is too good to let go. After all, geologist and gardener is a much more compatible relationship than that of lawyer and gardener. I think we should investigate the possibilities, don't you?' And, bending slowly, he planted a soft kiss on her swollen lips. Then, raising his head, he smiled into her wide, astonished eyes. 'No more games. Complete honesty between us from this moment forth.'

She was tempted to tell all but, lowering her lashes to disguise the guilt that shaded her golden eyes, she only murmured, 'I hope so.' Rocco was being so open, but she still had doubts.

'And, Marlene,' Rocco continued, 'Caterina did not have to tell me to seduce you. I decided to do it the moment I set eyes on you—for my own sake and nobody else's—and I hope to do it over and over and over again,' he opined in a husky drawl, and, sliding his hands from her shoulders down her back, he pulled her against him. Her breasts nestled against his chest and her gasp of surprise was swallowed by his mouth capturing hers in a long, hot kiss. Her doubts were going up in smoke as her temperature rose...

CHAPTER EIGHT

RELUCTANTLY Marlene raised her hands to his bare chest and pushed out of his embrace. 'Wait, Rocco,' she demanded breathlessly. She loved him too much to deceive him. He had to know about her real career, her primary reason for coming to Italy, the suspicions she had about Andretti. Obviously her informant had meant *Carlo* Andretti, and not the wonderful man in whose arms she lay. She was convinced of that...

'I know, I know,' he said, giving her a quick squeeze and then standing up. 'Paul will be awake any minute. I'll go and check on him.'

With a little space between them, Marlene's common sense returned and—coward that she was!—she leapt at the excuse he had given her to avoid the confession. 'Yes,' she agreed, with a wide smile that was part relief as well as pleasure. It could not hurt to delay a little longer, she told herself. Why upset their new relationship so soon? And telling the truth might well do that. Tucking the sheet firmly around her body, she began to get up, adding, 'And I'd better get dressed.'

'Stay where you are for an hour or so. I will amuse Paul,' Rocco drawled, his lips curling in a sensuous smile. 'I want you wide awake later; I fully intend to take up where we left off.'

'You're incorrigible,' she chuckled. 'But a siesta is out. I don't want Paul to find me in your bedroom,' she said, with a quick glance around the room, surprised to notice that it was almost the same as hers, but smaller.

'This isn't my room.' The sensual gleam in his eyes deepened as his large hand curved over her naked

shoulder and pushed her back. 'If you recall, we were
in rather a hurry to get into bed.' Marlene blushed bright
red at the reminder, and Rocco's grin widened. 'Your
bed was out, in case Paul walked in, so I simply carried
you to the room next door.' His gaze dropped from her
lovely face to her full breasts, sending a delicious shiver
of awareness through her body. He noticed, and added
wryly, 'And if I don't get out of here in the next second
I'll be back in the bed with you.'

'Promises, promises,' Marlene teased.

'Witch,' he shot back, and, placing a swift kiss on the
top of her head, he straightened up. 'Do as you're told
and have a rest.'

'As you command, O Master.' Marlene lay back, a
slumberous smile tilting her lips. Her eyes travelled over
his wide shoulders, down to his flat stomach and on to
where his shorts, open at the waist, clung perilously to
his lean hips. The promise of the night to come was
enough to make her stomach curl. A rest was a good
idea . . .

Rocco grinned down at her. 'Cheeky,' he said, and,
turning with a last glance around at the stark black and
white décor of the room, he added as he crossed to the
door, 'Mind you, all the rooms in this house look the
same. Awful. I can't imagine why anyone would want
the place.'

At the door he blew her a kiss, but Marlene had
already closed her eyes. She didn't see him leave. She
opened them when she heard the door close, and sighed.
What was the matter with her? Her emotions were all
over the place. One minute she was ready to reveal
everything to Rocco, then he made a simple comment
about the villa and she was immediately suspicious again.

Had he said the house was awful simply to make her
feel better about getting rid of it? He knew the deal she
had made with the Contessa was all in that lady's favour.
She had heard him arguing about it. Yet he had never

mentioned it to Marlene. Perhaps her secrets were best kept to herself for a little while longer... One afternoon of lovemaking did not necessarily mean that Rocco loved her.

Much later in the afternoon, with Paul quite happily playing in the pool with Rocco, Marlene, wearing her favourite denim shorts and a blue vest-top, sunned herself on a lounger, her eyes following the antics of the two males in her life with fond indulgence. Rocco certainly had a way with the boy, she mused, and it had been kind of him this morning to show Paul where he and his father used to go fishing. Talking about the other man as his friend had probably helped the little boy accept his father's death more than any grief counsellor ever could. It was funny to think of Paolo Rossi befriending Rocco; he must have been years older.

'Why the frown? Feeling neglected?' Rocco's deep, husky voice broke into her thoughts.

She looked up. He was standing at the foot of the lounger, beads of water glistening on his bronzed skin, all vibrant male, and without thinking she asked, 'How old are you?'

He gazed back at her, a warm, quizzical look in his eyes. 'Thirty-seven—but what brought that on?'

'Watching you with Paul.' She glanced around. 'Where is he?'

'Gone into the kitchen. But you haven't answered my question.' Pulling up a lounger, he sat on the side of it.

'I was thinking of your friendship with his father. Paolo must have been a lot older than you.' Marlene turned her head to look at him. A pensive, reminiscent glow lightened his dark eyes.

'Yes, he was, but he always had time for me—even when he was still single and sowing his wild oats. And by all accounts he was quite wild...' He chuckled, and with a shake of his dark head continued, 'But I remember that shortly after I had learnt about my father's infidelities Paolo came to stay with us. I had not seen him for a long time. He had been in England, I think, on business. He must have been around thirty then, and was already very successful.

'My father was his friend and lawyer, yet when I broke down and told Paolo what I had discovered, how I hated my father for hurting my mother and how it wasn't fair, he was marvellous. He had just got engaged to the Contessa at the time, but he took time to comfort me and explained that once I was grown up I would discover life wasn't fair. That a man could only try and do the best he could, and try not to hurt anyone in the process.'

'That's beautiful,' she said softly.

Rocco shrugged. 'Yes, maybe.' His mouth hardened. 'But it didn't stop Rossi doing exactly the same to his wife a few years later.' When Marlene stared at him he added deliberately, 'Never confuse great sex with love, that is my motto.'

As a warning it was very effective. She looked at him for a long, tense moment, before returning with a sarcasm she did not try to hide, 'And I suppose you have known both and never recognised either?' And, swinging her legs off the other side of the lounger, she made to stand up.

Rocco leaned forward and caught her arm, forcing her to remain seated.

'Let me go,' she said tonelessly.

He turned her to face him, his grip gentle but firm. 'I recognise I want you,' he said smoothly, his dark brown eyes searching her face. 'Marlene, look at me.'

She lifted her lashes, giving him a hard stare. A large hand touched her hair and brushed it from her brow almost tenderly, and she trembled. He smiled, and she thought how humiliatingly easy it was for him to bend her to his will. A simple touch...

'We want each other. Let's not spoil what we have by analysing every word we say, hmm?'

'I—yes, all right,' she heard herself agree meekly, and even more meekly lifted her head for his kiss.

'That's the second time you've kissed Mar. Does that mean you're getting married?' a little voice asked from behind the loungers.

'Good God, no!' Rocco exclaimed, standing up abruptly. 'I've kissed dozens of girls in my time. It didn't mean I was going to marry them.'

Marlene laughed out loud at the look of astonishment on Rocco's face, but inside her heart shrivelled a little. He had set the parameters of their relationship in no uncertain terms. A passionate affair...

She was suddenly very glad she had not told Rocco the whole truth. Her judgement was seriously affected by the man. After next Friday, and the board meeting, if he still wanted to see her, fine. But until then she would keep her own counsel. It was by far the safest way...

'Come on, Paul.' Rocco picked the little boy up in his arms. 'I can see you and I need to have a man-to-man talk, and at the same time we'll set up the barbecue.' Smiling down at Marlene, his expression bland, he added, 'And you, lady, get to the kitchen and make a salad. You have two hungry men on your hands.' Bending down, he kissed her—a fleeting, impersonal brush of his lips over hers. And yet it sent her emotions haywire.

How did he do that? she wondered, marching off towards the kitchen, masculine laughter following her every step of the way. And why did she let him? was her next furious thought as she strode inside.

A few minutes later, pulling lettuce leaves apart like a demented shrew, she had her answer when she looked out of the window. Rocco and Paul were placing pieces of charcoal on the barbecue in between throwing them at each other, and they were both getting filthy in the process. God help her! Because she loved him...

She stared sightlessly through the window, refusing to allow herself to feel sad... That way lay an anguish too deep to be borne. Instead she concentrated on the positive. For a few glorious days she could have Rocco, the man she loved, as her lover. It would have to be enough... Enough to last her through a lifetime of loneliness. Because she knew she would never love another man. Her mother had been a one-man woman and she knew she was the same...

Afterwards, back home in England, it might not be so bad. She had a brilliant career, and the family business had provided a very respectable income for almost half a century and would continue to do so. She would never know the wonder of giving birth to her own child, but she was luckier than most in that she had Paul. She had mothered him from a very young age, and all the pleasure of watching him grow and learn would be hers. Yes, she could do it...

Her gaze dropped down to the bench and the pile of mangled lettuce. Her mind was made up. She would take whatever Rocco had to offer. She was twenty-six, more than old enough to handle a sophisticated affair, and when they parted—as they surely must—she would walk away with her head held high, no regrets, no recriminations.

Swinging round with a new determination in her step, she opened the refrigerator and took out a bowl of tomatoes and a plate of juicy-looking steaks. When Rocco and Paul entered the kitchen five minutes later she was busily slicing tomatoes and looking as if she had not a care in the world. Only a very close observer would have noticed the shadow of restraint in her golden-brown eyes as she smiled brightly and said, 'Well, that's my part done. I'll leave the burning of the meat to you two.'

Dinner was a hilarious affair. Marlene insisted on her steak being so well done that Rocco grimaced in disgust when he finally plopped it on her plate.

'You weren't kidding when you talked about burning the meat. Do you honestly like burnt steak?'

She was seated at the glass-topped table on the terrace, with Paul beside her. The salad, bread, wine and condiments had all been lined up like a row of soldiers by Paul. She looked up at Rocco with a tilted head and a wicked smile. 'I'm a lady who likes everything well done,' she drawled, with conscious provocation.

He gazed back at her, a hot, predatory look in his eyes. 'I will remind you of that later,' he growled. And he did...

Marlene lay entangled with him, her limbs heavy, her eyelids drooping, stated in the aftermath of their loving. Rocco eased his weight away but held her to his hard body. Gradually the sensual haze drained away and Marlene attempted to move.

'What do you think you are doing?' Rocco murmured, his breath against her ear.

'I have to get back to my room. Paul wakes early—and don't forget Aldo and Eta will be back in the morning. I'm not sleeping with you when they're here.'

'Damn.' Rocco rolled over on his back and laced his fingers behind his head. 'I suppose you're right.'

Marlene leaned over him and pressed a last, lingering kiss to his lips. 'You know I am.' Her breasts pressing against his chest sent a renewed tremor of awareness shuddering through her, and she sighed. The pale light of dawn was already filtering through the window. She had to go.

He swooped with the speed of an eagle. His hand clasped her nape and he brought her mouth back down to meet his in a fierce, passionate kiss. 'Not yet,' he growled, and, grasping her around the waist, he lifted her over him.

Straddled across his muscular thighs, she moaned, her head falling back as his mouth found the rigid peak of her full breast and suckled fiercely while his hand rolled its partner between his fingers. 'We can't...' she tried to say.

But his hands curved round her buttocks and suddenly she was impaled by the hard, thrusting length of him. 'Your turn, Marlene. Ride me.' His black eyes burned up into hers and she slowly rotated her hips. Her golden eyes shooting flames, she bent forward and circled his mouth with her tongue in the same rhythm.

Time didn't matter. Nothing mattered, Marlene thought as once again she lost herself in the magic of the man. She did not recognise the woman she had become in Rocco's arms, but she gloried in the freedom to discover the wanton, demanding side of her nature. She was the one in control...

Pushing her hands against his chest, she arched back and held him still, allowing her slender fingers to scrape the small male nipples and then tease them as he had done to her while her long hair streamed down her back, brushing his thighs. But she wasn't in control for long...

'You want to play?' Rocco growled throatily, and suddenly his large hands linked around her slender waist. He held her in a grip of steel and bucked beneath her until he had taken her to the heights yet again.

Collapsed on top of him, touching him from shoulder to toes, her heart pounding, she breathed reluctantly, 'I must go.'

'Yes.' And a moment later he was carrying her naked in his arms back to her own room.

'I'm amazed you have the strength,' she whispered against his now rough jaw.

Rocco lowered her down on the bed and, pressing a last, light kiss to her brow, murmured softly, 'You give me the strength of ten men. Now go to sleep.' And silently he left the room.

Later that morning Marlene, glowing from her night of passion, supervised Paul's breakfast with one eye on him and the other on the door, anticipating Rocco's appearance. She had just filled Paul's glass with orange juice for the third time when Rocco walked into the kitchen.

She glanced up. His bronzed, perfectly carved features were relaxed in a wide smile. His tall, muscular body was clad in a black shirt that emphasised the natural width of his shoulders and well-washed denim jeans that clung to his lean hips and thighs. Suddenly she could see him as a geologist, prospecting in out-of-the-way places. He looked like a modern-day cowboy—quite the reverse of the sartorial elegance he displayed when Caterina and the Contessa were around. She could not control the leaping of her pulse as her eyes met his. He looked good enough to eat...

'Rocco, did you sleep well?' Nervously she burst into speech. Even after the intimacy they had shared she was still not sure how to behave; she had very little experience in morning-after protocol. Did she pretend it hadn't happened? Or throw herself in his arms and demand more? But Rocco solved her problem...

He threw his head back and laughed out loud. 'Like a log, sweetheart.' And in two lithe strides he was beside her, bending to press a kiss to her parted lips. 'How could you doubt it after last night?' he queried, his dark eyes looking tenderly down into hers, dispelling all her doubts.

'You look different this morning. I think it's the jeans,' she opined. 'Not your usual mode of dress...' she babbled on, and he stopped her with another kiss.

'Shows how little you know me. The Contessa, as you have learnt, demands a certain standard. I did try to explain that day in Amalfi, but you took it the wrong way.' Marlene remembered their argument about manners. 'When she's around it is easier to comply than argue. She turns puce at the sight of a man or woman in jeans.' And, mimicking the Contessa's voice remarkably well, he added, 'Jeans are for workmen, and not to be worn in the house.'

Marlene laughed, thrilled to learn yet another facet of Rocco's intriguing character. 'So really you're just as much of a slob as I am?' She grinned, and was rewarded with yet another kiss.

'You kissed Mar again!' Paul exclaimed, and, screwing up his little face, added, 'Ugh—sloppy.'

'Boy, have you got a lot to learn.' Rocco turned his attention to Paul. 'Hurry up and finish your breakfast. I'm taking you and Marlene to my home today.'

'Are you, now? And do I have any say in the matter?' Marlene demanded easily.

'Not if you want me again,' he breathed in her ear, sending a delicious shiver down her spine, as he brushed past her around the table to where the coffee-percolator stood on the bench.

'Devil,' Marlene murmured under her breath at his broad back—but not quietly enough, apparently.

Turning, Rocco winked—he knew very well what he did to her—then took a cup from the rack and poured himself a cup of coffee. 'Aldo and Eta have just arrived. I heard their car pull up as I dressed. We'll wait and say hello and then take off.' And, draining his coffee-cup, he replaced it on the bench. Grinning at her scarlet complexion, he walked around the table to where she still stood. 'I seem to remember you saying last night you wouldn't sleep with me with Aldo and Eta in the house,' he drawled huskily. 'I'm giving you an alternative.'

Trapped by the sensual gleam in his dark eyes, Marlene had great difficulty recalling anything. Even so, half an hour later she found herself seated next to Rocco in his low-slung sports car with Paul strapped into the back seat. Beside him was a bag containing their swimwear, a few toys and Rocco's weekend case.

'You could have moved in with me,' Rocco said, slanting her a glance as he manoeuvred the car down the twisting road. 'It would have been much easier. My housekeeper and her husband are on holiday for the summer. We'd have had absolute privacy.'

'I told you—no. Think how it would look to Paul—and don't forget your father. He's coming out to the villa one day this week with some papers for me to sign.' They had already had this argument earlier, when, after greeting Aldo and Eta, Rocco had followed her up to her room and suggested she pack everything and stay at his place. Marlene had been tempted, but common sense had prevailed and she had refused.

'Have it your own way,' Rocco muttered, and then, his mood brightening, he shot her a wicked grin. 'Love in the afternoon it is.'

Marlene's eyes widened in wonder as the car slipped through a stone arch set in a high wall completely covered in vividly coloured creepers and a profusion of brightly coloured flowers. They stopped in a paved courtyard before a long, low stucco-washed house with a mellow terracotta roof. The white and pink of oleanders and geraniums tumbled from windowsills and dozens of hanging baskets...even the chimney was covered with purple clematis.

'Welcome to my home,' Rocco said formally as he opened the car door for her to alight, then scooped Paul, bag and all, out of the back seat.

She stood up and simply stared. It was exactly as she imagined a Mediterranean villa should look. The contrast with the stark, barrack-like lines of the Rossi villa was incredible.

'Do you like it?' The question was almost hesitant.

She lifted glowing eyes up to his. 'It is beautiful—the most beautiful house I have ever seen,' she said. And it was.

Steps led up to a covered terrace supported by a row of Moorish arches covered in vines of every description. They walked up the steps and across the terrace to where a heavy arched door opened into the house. The hall stretched from front to back, with a corridor leading off either side. The floor was a brilliant blue and white marble mosaic, with a circle in the middle enclosing a marvellously mosaic picture of the god Bacchus. At the rear large French windows opened onto the garden beyond.

'Bacchus?' she queried, arching one delicate brow. 'A bit naughty.'

'Not at all. I told you—the house belonged to my mother's family; they were brewers and also kept a vineyard not far from here. I'll let you sample a bottle later, if you're good.'

'I always am,' she joked, looking up at him, and was stunned by the glitter of naked desire she saw in the depths of his eyes. A flash of awareness shot through her, frightening in its intensity.

'God! Don't I know it,' he husked; then, as if remembering they were not alone, he swallowed hard and continued calmly, 'To the right are the reception rooms, kitchen and utilities, and to the left the bedroom suites.'

With Paul in one arm, he took her hand in his and led her along the corridor to the left. He stopped outside the first door, and with a quick squeeze of her hand let her go. Opening the door, he indicated the room with a tilt of his dark head. 'You can change in here, but feel free to explore the place. Unfortunately I have a few calls to make, but I'll catch up with you later in the garden.'

Marlene looked around the room and smiled. It was charming. It had obviously been a young boy's room at some time. A single bed with a carved polished oak headboard stood at one side of the window, on the other side a matching wardrobe and desk. The furniture was old but classical. What really gave the game away was a long-forgotten poster of some footballer over the bed and a collection of pennants strung along the whitewashed wall. Somehow she could see Rocco as a young boy, spending his summers here.

With a delighted sigh, she swiftly divested Paul of his clothes and got him into his bathing trunks. Equally quickly she shed her shorts and shirt and slipped into her swimsuit. 'Come on.' She took Paul's hand. 'Let's explore.' And they did.

They headed straight for the French doors and the garden. A paved area led to a few steps down to a green lawn. It must take gallons of water to keep it so fresh in this heat, Marlene thought as they walked down the gentle slope to where another few steps led to the next level.

Here the mosaic of the hall was repeated in a huge square. In the centre of the square a shallow pool fed a waterfall that tumbled about two feet over rocks into a large circular swimming pool, the bottom of which sported another mosaic, this time of the god Neptune. It was obviously quite old, but in tip-top condition. It reminded Marlene of pictures she had seen of Roman baths, even down to the steps in the side that led gently into the sparkling water. There was no danger to a child here. Paul could quite happily play in the shallow pool when he got tired of swimming.

At one side there was a row of three changing cabins, and at the other a few loungers set around a low stone table. Beyond the pool the garden dropped again, in row upon row of shallow terraces which were covered in a mass of shrubs and flowers of every scent and hue. Dotted about were ancient stone sculptures, weathered by time, that looked like the gods of legend. The garden ended on a small sandy beach with the turquoise water of the Mediterranean flowing away to the distant horizon. Enclosed on both sides by rocky headlands, it was completely private and perfect.

Marlene stood for a moment, savouring the peace and perfection, and had a moment's regret that she had not agreed to move in here with Rocco. But she did not have time to dwell on it as Paul demanded her attention.

Later, as she lay on a lounger keeping one eye on Paul playing happily in the pool, she heard Rocco call her name.

She watched him approach, unaware of the hungry gleam in her golden eyes. He moved with an easy grace that was unusual in such a large man. His tanned, muscular physique was a picture of perfect symmetry—a joy to behold. She sat up on the lounger, unconsciously licking her bottom lip as her eyes roamed over him. Today he was wearing slightly more conservative swimming shorts in plain black, but nothing could disguise his masculine perfection.

'Shut your mouth—you're drooling, sweetheart,' he declared outrageously, and dropped down to sit on the ground at her feet.

Marlene blushed from head to toe. 'Think of Paul...' she spluttered.

'No, thanks, I don't fancy him,' he quipped, and, wrapping his hand around her ankle, he slowly stroked up her leg. 'But you! You I *do* fancy. I am at your feet— what more could a woman want?' he asked mockingly.

'Fool! Get up!' she exclaimed. His hand had reached the back of her knee and it was doing impossible things to her breathing.

'Oh, that I could,' he said, and, jumping to his feet, leant over her, so only she could hear, and told her exactly what he would like to get up to.

'Rocco...' She murmured his name, her slender hands reaching up to clasp his biceps, the blood hot in her veins.

'Soon, very soon,' he told her, and, devilment lurking in his eyes, he swept her up in his arms. 'But first I need to cool you down and then make sure Paul will be tired enough to take a nap.'

Flinging her arms around his neck, she cried, 'No, don't you dare!' But he did. He dropped her in the big pool, and she hit the water with an almighty splash. She surfaced, spluttering and choking, to see Paul and Rocco standing on the waterfall, laughing their heads off...

Later, when they were all dried and dressed again, Rocco provided a light meal of salad and grilled fish in the small breakfast room that led off a typical country kitchen. He introduced Marlene to a local wine—not the best-known wine of the area, Lacryma Christi, but a delicious sparkling Liquoroso that was made in his own vineyard. Later still he carried a sleepy Paul back to the little bedroom and watched as Marlene tucked a fine sheet over the little boy.

'Do you want another drink? A coffee?' Rocco asked rather formally.

She looked up at him as she closed the door on the sleeping child. He was watching her, his dark eyes intent, and was that a flash of vulnerability she saw in his gaze? 'A siesta would be nice,' she said boldly, her heart in her eyes.

Pulling her into his arms, Rocco murmured, 'You give so generously, how could I ever have thought you were mercenary?' He groaned throatily and covered her mouth with his.

She might have been annoyed at his remark, but with his whole length pressed against her and his mouth doing wonderful things to her lips, her eyes, her throat all conscious thought left her as she became a slave to her passionate emotions. He swung her off her feet, his mouth once more on hers, and she closed her eyes, her arms around his neck. She didn't see the bed, she only felt it at her back, and his large body over her...

That day set the pattern for the next two days. Rocco took Marlene and Paul back to the Rossi villa at night, shared dinner with them and then left, to return early the next morning and whisk them back to his home.

They spent the mornings playing in the pool, and in the afternoons, when Paul was asleep, Rocco carried Marlene off to the wide bed in the master bedroom, where they indulged themselves in an orgy of love-making. When they talked the conversation was light-hearted—the kind of stupid things lovers say. They consciously avoided the real reason for Marlene's being in Italy. Neither one of them was prepared to upset their idyllic existence...

On Wednesday night the idyll was broken...

'Come back and eat your ice cream,' Marlene remonstrated with Paul. They were eating out on the patio and Paul had slid off his chair and was trying to catch the fireflies dancing around in the soft, scented night air.

'Let him be,' Rocco murmured, reaching across the table to take her hand gently in his. 'I used to try and catch them as a child, but I rarely did. He will soon tire.'

'Yes, when the ice cream is a pool of cream,' Marlene opined with a wry smile. 'You spoil the boy.'

'But of course.' He chuckled. 'I want to keep in with his sister.' And, lifting her hand to his lips, he pressed a tender kiss to her soft palm. Marlene marvelled anew at the flush of pleasure his lightest caress gave her, and was about to tell him so when Eta appeared.

'Signorina Marlene, telephone for you—it is Signor Andretti.'

Rocco dropped her hand, his expression suddenly remote. 'You'd better answer it.'

Returning to the terrace five minutes later, Marlene saw that Paul was back at the table and eating his ice cream. She resumed her seat beside him and studied her plate, not sure what to tell Rocco.

'So what did the old man want?' Rocco asked lightly, breaking the awkward silence. 'Obviously not to speak to me.'

Marlene shot him a surprised glance. He seemed remarkably unconcerned. 'No, you weren't mentioned,' she said quietly. 'He has the agreement drawn up for the Contessa to buy out Paul's interest in the villa. He's calling here tomorrow at noon for my signature.'

'No doubt you'll be pleased to get it all settled at last.'

'Yes.' She waited, wondering if at last they would have a frank discussion about the business that had brought her here. But to her astonishment he simply looked at her and smiled.

'Good, but not so good,' Rocco drawled ruefully. 'No more love in the afternoon!'

Marlene's heart leapt with hope. Now he was going to tell her she was being ripped off—prove his loyalty to her, and maybe his love. But with his next words the spark of hope withered in her breast.

'But as it happens I have to go to Rome tomorrow anyway. I've been offered the opportunity to lecture in geology at a top university—a sabbatical from fieldwork—and I am seriously considering accepting. I'll be staying overnight, so you and my father will have plenty of time to sort out your business without me getting in the way.'

'He also wants to discuss the company shares I hold,' she couldn't help adding. The news that Rocco was leaving for two days was bad. She might never see him again, and she prayed that now he would show in some small way that he was interested in her business and not just leave her at his father's mercy. Surely if Rocco cared anything at all for her as a person, and not just a body in his bed, he would want to protect her and Paul's interests? The past four days they had spent together must mean something to him, she thought desperately... But she was instantly disillusioned.

'Marlene, you're an intelligent woman. You run your family business successfully; you speak Italian well. Get rid of the shares or attend the board meeting first, if you must. Either way, I'm sure you'll make the right decision.'

'You think so?' she asked, mollified slightly by his faith in her even if she was furious at his lack of support.

'Of course. But get it settled. I want nothing to upset our meeting again on Friday night. We can make it a celebration.' His intimate gaze slid over her blonde head, down to where the soft curves of her breasts were displayed by the ubiquitous yellow mini-dress and then back to her face.

'I don't know exactly what time I'll be back—early evening, probably. But I'll leave you the key to my house and arrange for Aldo to drive you over.' Putting his hand in his trouser pocket, he withdrew a key and put it on the table in front of her. 'You and Paul can spend your last night there, and I'll join you.' He curved his hard mouth into a confident smile, sure she would agree.

He had it all planned. He couldn't care less if she lost a fortune so long as she was there to share his bed one last time. The smug swine, she thought bitterly, and if she could have reached him she would have punched him. It was only by a terrific effort of will that she refrained from throwing her coffee in his face.

But she had her answer, she thought grimly. Rocco had no real feeling for her. He was a virile man and she was a convenient body to while away a few hours with— nothing more. He might say he didn't get on with his father, but his loyalty was to his family and friends, not to her. Yet he still had the arrogance, the audacity to say there would be no more love in the afternoon, so how about spending her last night in Italy in his home and in his bed?

'And I suppose you'll give my brother and me a lift to the airport Saturday morning?' she prompted sarcastically. She was longing to say more, but with Paul at the table she had to restrain her temper.

'We'll see about that when the time comes.' Rocco grinned.

No doubt he would quite happily shove them in a taxi with a quick goodbye and good riddance, she imagined. But she never knew what she might have said next in her anger, for at that moment Eta arrived to clear the table, and she was left speechless with amazement as Rocco casually proceeded to arrange with the woman for Aldo to take Marlene and Paul to his home on Friday afternoon.

She watched, silently fuming, as Eta walked away with a loaded tray of dishes, and wondered why she had taken the key Eta had picked up off the table and handed to her.

'There you are, Marlene, all arranged.'

'I never said yes,' she got out between clenched teeth.

'But you were going to.' Rocco stood up and walked around to place his large hands on her shoulders. She tried to shake him off but he began massaging the knot of tension between her shoulderblades. 'Relax, sweetheart. Let me work it out,' and bending low, he brushed the top of her head with his lips.

'Ugh! You're getting sloppy again. I want to go to bed,' Paul piped up, and Marlene jumped at the chance to get away from Rocco. Shrugging off his hands, she got to her feet. She picked Paul up out of his chair and swung him into her arms. Holding him in front of her, she turned and raised her head, and was caught and held by the intensity of Rocco's glittering gaze.

'I'm taking Paul to bed.' She said the first thing that came into her head, stating the obvious.

'I can see that.' His lips quirked in a gentle smile, and to her surprise he added, 'You look wonderful with a child in your arms.'

'Oh,' Marlene said, totally ineptly. 'Yes, well...goodnight.'

'Is something wrong?' he demanded, and, raising one hand, he lightly tapped her cheek. 'You seem rather flustered.'

He had finally realised she was not the willing woman who had spent the afternoon in his arms, in his bed. He had to be the most insensitive jerk in the universe, she told herself, and opened her mouth to tell him so. But she was stopped by his lips pressing briefly against hers.

'You're tired. The pair of you go to bed. I'll see you the day after tomorrow.' And then, brushing a few stray strands of hair from her brow, he added, 'I won't come in with you. I may get distracted by the bedrooms.' With a grin, he spun on his heel and strolled towards the side of the house, where a flight of stone steps cut into the rock led to the top and the road.

CHAPTER NINE

MARLENE stood on the terrace and watched his departing back. Suddenly he halted and slowly turned. The white light of the halogen lamps starkly revealed his handsome features, highlighting the intensity of his dark gaze as it clashed with hers.

For a long, tense moment he simply stared at her with the boy in her arms. Then he shook his head, as if to clear it, and said, 'Friday night is important. Be waiting for me, Marlene.' And to her astonishment he added, 'I will take care of everything—trust me.' Then, turning, he disappeared around the side of the house with the speed of light.

Marlene spent a restless night, her emotions fluctuating wildly between anger at Rocco's high-handed attitude, being convinced it was all over between them, and a desperate yearning to be back in his arms. The next morning she awoke with a splitting headache. It was not improved when she cast a quick glance out of the window to discover that the brilliant sunshine of the past few days had been replaced by a ferocious summer storm. Black clouds rolled over the sky, lightning flashed and torrential rain splattered down the window. A portent for the day ahead, she thought drily.

An hour later, with Paul safely ensconced in the kitchen with a colouring book and Eta's watchful eye on him, Marlene was seated in the study, the telephone pressed to her ear. What she heard was music to her ears. Her contact in England confirmed that it was a Mr *Carlo* Andretti who had been buying shares in Rossi International at a knock-down price. But she had nothing to worry about. A broker colleague had followed her instructions to the letter, and with the help of a handful of her clients a further seven per cent of Rossi stock had been bought. The voting proxies in her name would arrive by the evening, giving her thirty-one per cent of the overall vote at tomorrow's board meeting.

The icing on the cake was the name and address of a Signor Toni in Amalfi, who might be able to help her further. The man held twenty per cent of the stock. Apparently years ago, when Paolo Rossi had started the company, Signor Toni had lent him some money and had been made a silent partner in the business. According to Marlene's informant, Signor Toni was loyal to his late friend and had refused all offers to sell.

Another telephone call, and then ten minutes later Marlene and Paul were in the back of the Mercedes, being driven into Amalfi by the demon driver Aldo! Marlene was not sure how far she could trust Aldo. He seemed pleasant enough, but she didn't dare make a mistake at this late stage. So she instructed him to drop them off at the port and call back in two hours. He looked at her rather oddly, but obeyed.

Finding the house of Signor Toni was simple—the first person she asked took her to the door. She had to smile when she met him. He was the local undertaker, and looked the exact opposite: small and round, with a cherub-like face and rosy red complexion, and his beaming smile was irresistible. He took one look at Marlene and Paul, and tears of emotion slid down his cheeks.

'Come in, come in out of the rain,' he urged, and, ushering them into his house, turned and said, 'He is so like his father. It does my heart good to see him at last.'

'You knew!' Marlene exclaimed.

'Of course... Paolo was my oldest friend and con- fided in me. I also know he was your father as well. You have his eyes.'

'Yes,' Marlene said simply, taking the chair that was offered her. 'I only found out myself a few months ago. My mother had always taught me what a good man my "father" was—the man she married—and apparently did not have the courage to disillusion me later. Paolo didn't agree, but he loved my mother so much he promised her he wouldn't tell me. But he left a letter for me to read after his death, explaining everything and telling me how much he loved me.'

It was a relief to Marlene to be able to talk honestly at last, and over a cup of coffee Signor Toni gave her an insight into her natural father's life as a young boy, with several hilarious anecdotes and some not so funny. Then they got down to business...

Almost two hours later the old man kissed her on both cheeks when she left, and promised to be waiting for her in the morning. Marlene was ecstatic. Success was assured. Even the weather had cleared up and the sun shone bright and clear once more. She had done it! Well, just about, she qualified as Aldo stopped the car outside the villa again and she saw that Signor Andretti had already arrived.

It was not a pleasant interview. Seated in the study behind the large desk, Signor Andretti was in charge—or thought he was. Marlene, on the other hand, knew differently, but she forced herself not to show her true feelings. Instead, with a smile, she signed away Paul's right to the villa. She felt a slight stab of regret—according to Rocco, this piece of land had been in the Rossi family for decades—but looking around, she recognised that the Contessa had destroyed any trace of Rossi influence with the stark ugliness of the building.

But the woman was not going to get the chance to do the same to the Rossi name, Marlene vowed, and, playing her part of a simple country woman, she resisted all Signor Andretti's demands to sell her shares in the company.

Oddly enough, she realised that the man still did not know she spoke Italian. As she had given up pretending since Rocco had found out on Sunday, Aldo and Eta also knew now. Obviously Signor Carlo Andretti was no closer to his son than he was to servants. Unless Rocco had been deliberately quiet on her account. If so, she silently thanked him for it. It made her task so much easier. His father took her for a stupid woman and that was his mistake, and the more she refused to sell, the more aggressive he got. He even had the gall to wave another cheque in her face. But she could not help noticing he had not upped the price from the original two pounds a share that Rocco had offered her in England.

Finally, after she had listened to the man go on and on about the advisability of selling her shares, she got to her feet. 'No, Signor Andretti, I'm sorry. I'm hanging onto them. Who knows? They might go up in price after tomorrow's board meeting.' She could not resist the sly dig. She knew perfectly well that the price was already rising after her intervention in the market.

For one awful moment she thought he was going to have a fit. His eyes bulged and his fat face turned scarlet. He really was nothing at all like his son. The inconsequential thought fluttered in her mind, but quickly vanished under the barrage of abuse he heaped upon her before storming out. In a fierce, low voice he grated in Italian, not expecting her to understand, 'You're a mercenary, gold-digging little bitch. I hope you and your bastard brother rot in hell.'

Marlene collapsed back on the chair she had just vacated, shaking with shock. Never had she suffered such abuse and, taking slow, deep breaths, she struggled to regain some semblance of control. With control came an icy, bone-deep anger...

Never mind being Paolo's lawyer, Signor Carlo Andretti was supposed to have been a lifelong friend of the man, and yet she knew without a shadow of a doubt that it was he and the Contessa who, over the past few months, had deliberately started the rumours which had made the share price drop. And it was Carlo Andretti who had bought at rock-bottom prices. The only part she could not make any sense of was why the Contessa would deliberately try to ruin her own husband's business and so decrease her own income. Unless the woman was simple or crazy, Marlene thought, and, getting to her feet, glanced around. Or both! Anyone who could design a house like this had to be . . .

And, come tomorrow, she was not going to be welcome here, so she might as well spend the afternoon packing. With Paul in bed for his nap, she opened the wardrobe door, and pulled the two suitcases out of the bottom. She carried them to the bed and stopped, suddenly remembering how she had spent the last few afternoons in Rocco's bed. She shuddered, her body flushing with heat at the memories. Then she noticed his key on the bedside table, where she had dropped it last night. She picked it up and turned it slowly in her hand. He had given her the key to his house, but it was the key to his heart she really wanted. Or just his loyalty would have done, she thought resentfully, and, swinging around, she headed for the door.

She didn't want to think about Rocco or his love-making; she didn't want to think at all. A walk in the fresh air was what she needed.

But it didn't help. She passed the swimming pool and it brought back another memory, of a passionate underwater embrace. Shaking her head, Marlene strolled down to the lower terrace. She looked out to sea. The usually calm waters were dark and turbulent, white horses riding the waves. Her own emotions were equally turbulent.

She loved Rocco, and she knew he was not directly involved with the troubles at Rossi International. By his own admission he had only returned from South Africa a fortnight ago. She should have told him the whole truth about herself, trusted him. Last night he had said 'trust me' but she had been too angry at what she saw as his betrayal. Perhaps if she had told him everything he might have appreciated her point of view. But she hadn't given him the chance. After all, Rocco had his own life, his own career, she rationalised.

An image of them naked in bed, sated in the aftermath of loving, sipping wine and lazily talking filled her mind. He had spilt some on her breast and lapped it off. She had laughed and told him to behave and his response had been that he couldn't help it. He was a basic, earthy type of man. He owned the vineyard and a lot more, but, though he enjoyed the physical labour involved on occasion, and the profit, he was a firm believer in employing the best accountants and business managers, leaving him free to follow his first love—geology. He was in Rome now, doing just that, Marlene acknowledged.

She was clutching at straws, she knew. But was it really so terrible of him to leave her to sort out her own business? Rocco had approached her in the first place at the request of his father. By his own admission it had simply been because he had felt he should try and mend the breach between them, not because he had any vital interest in the affair himself. Last night it had seemed as if he had faith in her. So why had she been so angry? Wryly she finally admitted to herself that her anger and resentment had more to do with the shock of hearing that Rocco was leaving for two days than anything else.

Perhaps there was still a chance for them—and the only way to find out was to use his key tomorrow. She opened her hand and turned the big old key over in her palm, studying it, as if it could somehow give her an answer.

Suddenly the sun burst through a break in the clouds, covering Marlene with its warm embrace. Her hand tightened into a fist and she tilted her head back to look up at the sky. It was an omen, she thought. She was a fighter—always had been. She had spent her childhood without a father, but with lots of happy memories of him which her mother had instilled in her. All false, as it turned out...

She had overcome the hurtful gossip when her mother had taken a lover. She had pulled herself around after her mother's death and had happily taken charge of her brother. In business, with no false modesty, she knew that she was dynamite. And in the past few months she had reconciled herself to the biggest shock of all. That Paolo Rossi was her natural father. His death had been a double blow. Now she was fighting for his good name. By the same token she was going to fight for the man she loved. Rocco had left the key to his home, and tomorrow, after the board meeting, she was going to use it.

Turning, she headed back up the steps, her mind made up. Anyway, she thought with a wry smile, by tomorrow afternoon she would certainly be *persona non grata* in this place. Spending the last night at Rocco's made sense. When he discovered what she had done he would either kill her or kiss her. Either way she was going to take the chance...

The next morning her heart briefly picked up speed as she thought of the battle ahead. Very soon she would be in her natural element again—in the world of business—fighting for her father's name and almost certainly winning. The proxies she needed had arrived by special delivery last night; she had nothing to worry about.

Standing under the shower spray, she smoothed soap over her arms and around her full breasts. Unexpectedly her stomach curled as she recalled Rocco's hands doing the exact same thing. God, how she wanted him! With a shake of her head she dispelled the erotic images invading her mind, finished her shower and washed and dried her hair. Walking back into the bedroom with a large fluffy towel wrapped around her body, she skirted the packed suitcases standing in the middle of the floor and crossed to the wardrobe. A holdall with enough clothes for an overnight stay and a suit hanging on the rail were all it contained.

Paul was downstairs with Eta. Marlene had explained to him that she had to leave him for the morning but would be back for lunch, and that afterwards they were going to stay at Rocco's before returning to England. Paul had accepted the idea quite happily, saying that he liked Roc's house better, that the swimming pool was the best...

Marlene heartily agreed, only wishing she had Paul's same sunny disposition. She had hardly slept a wink all night, tossing and turning in the wide bed. Images of Rocco and the time they had spent together had filled her mind, and filled her body with the ache of frustration.

Taking a deep breath, she surveyed herself in the full-length mirror and a tiny smile curled her full lips. Gone was the casual blonde of the past two weeks and in her place was Marlene Johanson the business executive.

She wore a Donna Karan suit—a smart cream linen short-sleeved tailored jacket, nipped in at the waist, which fitted her like a glove, teamed with a short straight black skirt that ended two inches above her knee. Sheer silk stockings covered her long legs, and on her feet were black Italian leather shoes with three-inch heels, increasing her height to six feet.

Her blonde hair was swept up and round in a smooth French pleat—not a hair out of place. Her make-up was simple but perfect. In her ears she wore plain gold Christian Dior earrings, and on the lapel of her jacket was a matching brooch. To complete her ensemble, she picked up her handbag along with a practical black leather briefcase.

She said goodbye to Paul in the kitchen and grinned at the look of stunned amazement on the faces of Aldo and Eta. Aldo was still casting surreptitious glances at her five minutes later as he helped her into the car, and when she directed him to stop at Signor Toni's in Amalfi he simply nodded.

The boardroom of Rossi International was on the top floor of a lovely old building in the heart of Naples' business sector. Signor Toni gallantly took her elbow as they followed a smartly dressed man, who had been introduced as the company secretary, through the large double doors to the boardroom beyond. Marlene stopped just inside the entrance and coolly looked around. A typical boardroom, she thought. All panelled mahogany and large elegant windows draped in the finest Genoa velvet. There was a huge table laid with blotters, writing materials and glasses for the water and wine on offer. No one had yet taken a seat, she noted, and wondered who would chair the meeting.

Her glance went further, to the bottom of the room, where there was a magnificent marble mantelpiece with an excellent portrait of the late Paolo Rossi above it. But it was the group standing there that gave her pause. She recognised the Contessa, Caterina and Carlo Andretti, and there were also four men whose names she had in her possession but whom she had never met before. One, she knew, would be the company accountant.

'*Buongiorno*, Contessa, are we ready to start?' Marlene asked in fluent Italian. And she almost burst out laughing at the look of astonishment on the older woman's face, and on those around her.

'You speak Italian!' she exclaimed.

Marlene nodded, holding the black eyes with her own glittering gold ones. 'Are we ready to start?' she repeated. 'I want this business settled quickly.' She was a commanding figure, stunningly attractive, all efficiency, and it helped that she was the tallest person present.

'No, we are waiting for two more members,' the Contessa shot back, recovering some of her self-control. 'And what are you doing here, Signor Toni? You never usually bother.'

'I am here to protect my investment. What else?' He shrugged nonchalantly. 'Oh! And we can start. The other two members have sold their shares.' Signor Toni took great delight in telling the Contessa this, and Marlene did not begrudge him the privilege. In fact she had arranged it with him on the way here.

It was ludicrously simple in the end. After the preliminaries were over, and the company secretary took the chair in place of the late Paolo Rossi, the Contessa took the floor and gave a long speech on how badly the company shares were performing. She suggested the name of Rossi be discredited, and put forward a motion to reorganise and rename the company. Signor Andretti seconded the motion, and then Marlene rose to speak...

In a few short sentences she revealed her findings, and the paperwork to back them up. The assets of the company were vastly underrated. It was the Contessa who had deliberately started the rumours, in all the right places, with the sole purpose of lowering the share price and panicking people into selling. In the meantime, Signor Andretti had quietly been buying them at a rock-bottom price through a number of holding companies— all of which had been set up with the intention of gaining overall control. Why the Contessa wanted to change the name of the company Marlene had no idea. And she let her gaze linger on each man present individually for a moment at this point, before succinctly pointing out that the Contessa had caused their holdings to be greatly devalued.

Pandemonium broke out. The vote was a foregone conclusion. Marlene, with Signor Toni's vote and the votes of two of the other men, who had obviously known nothing about the conspiracy, easily outvoted the Contessa and her cronies. The company accountant was dismissed on the spot—it was obvious he was involved—and details on how to proceed were thrashed out without any trouble. The Contessa appeared to have been struck dumb, as did Andretti, and the meeting began to break up.

Marlene told Signor Toni in an aside that she was going to find the toilet, and left the boardroom. Crossing the hall, she found the door marked 'Donne'. She walked into the powder room and, standing in front of the vanity basin, glanced at her reflection in the mirror. Her eyes were sparkling, her face flushed; she looked triumphant and she was... Suddenly another face appeared in the mirror, and she spun around to confront the Contessa.

The Contessa looked right through Marlene as though she wasn't there. But Marlene had one more niggling problem, and she could not rest until she had it solved.

'Tell me, Contessa, why did you do it? Why set out to discredit the name of Rossi? Your own daughter's name—your name, even though you never use it. What possible reason could you have? You are a shareholder in a hugely successful company that keeps you in luxury. I simply cannot understand why.'

The Contessa's face was frightening to watch. 'I tell you why.' Her dark eyes gleaming malevolently, she stared at Marlene. 'I hated him. I hated Paolo Rossi from the day I married him.'

Marlene clutched the vanity basin, white-knuckled with shock. The woman meant it. It was in her face. 'But...'

'You don't know, do you? You are just like him, with your golden-brown eyes, your superb business brain. But naïve...'

'You knew he was my father!' Marlene exclaimed.

The Contessa threw her head back and laughed out loud, the laughter verging on hysteria. 'You stupid girl— I knew before you were born. That surprises you?' She cackled again. 'Rossi was in England, sleeping with your mother. I...I was madly in love with Carlo Andretti— a man of breeding, good pedigree, but no money—and he was married, with a child. A divorce was out of the question. I was pregnant, so we planned it between us.'

Her black eyes were venomous as she continued, 'Rossi came back to Italy full of his success in opening a London office, and Carlo invited him to stay at his home. He gave a party for him and I was a weekend guest. We got him drunk and a little more besides. The next morning he woke up in bed with me. He could remember nothing. Two weeks later I told him I was pregnant and he had to marry me. He wrote to your mother, breaking off the relationship, but Carlo had already intercepted a letter from her telling Rossi she was pregnant. Yes, I knew...'

As the implications of what the Contessa was saying sank in Marlene's eyes widened in horror. She had once likened the woman to Lucretia Borgia, and now she knew she'd been right. 'Then Caterina is...'

'I had to sleep with Paolo Rossi when I married him, but as soon as my child was born—ten weeks premature—' again she cackled '—I never let the man touch me again. Caterina is Carlo's daughter, but it is a secret. No one knows.' Giving Marlene a sly glance, she added, 'Not even Caterina. Promise—you have to promise not to tell.'

The woman was evil personified, Marlene thought, but still she told her what she wanted to hear. 'I promise no one will learn your secret from me.'

'Good, good. We should have been together, you know. We should have been a family. We should have had all the wealth.' As Marlene watched the Contessa's eyes seemed to lose their focus, gazing into some distant reality only she could see. The woman was mad, or very near it. 'And we nearly did. Carlo's wife died—did you know?' She turned back to Marlene, suddenly almost normal.

'Yes, I had heard,' Marlene said softly, humouring her.

'But she left all her wealth to Rocco, and he is too much like his mother. She was a brewer's daughter—no breeding . . . The fortune should have been Carlo's; she cheated him out of his rightful share. Poor Carlo. So I vowed to give him the wealth and status he should have.' She gave Marlene a cunning look. 'That was when I started my plan. I move in the highest echelons of society—a word to a banker here, an investment house there... It was easy. When the share price dropped Carlo quietly bought shares. We had it all worked out. Gain complete control, get rid of the hated name Rossi and replace it with Andretti. Then Carlo and I would marry.'

The amazing part was that it almost made sense, Marlene thought sadly. It all fitted. In the letter Paolo had left Marlene to read after his death he had explained how hurt he had been that her mother had never written to him, that if she had he might not have married the Contessa, baby or no. Of course he had never heard from her—because he had been staying in the home of Carlo Andretti and had never got the letter. Rocco had told her that he was about ten when he'd discovered his mother in tears at his father's infidelity. That was when the affair must have started. The time-scale fitted perfectly. Twenty-seven years later, and again the dates fitted. Paolo had noticed the trouble starting in the company a few months before he died. Just about the time when Rocco's mother had died, or very shortly after.

'He will marry me, you know.' The Contessa grabbed Marlene's arm and stared up into her face. 'The other women all meant nothing to Carlo. He did it to keep suspicion from falling on me.' And as Marlene watched in wide-eyed horror the Contessa ranted on. 'I did the same. I took one young lover because he was an architect. He was good—he did what I told him.' Another horrible cackle erupted from her mouth. 'He rebuilt the villa, destroying every trace of my hateful husband's common family.' She let go of Marlene's arm. 'And the villa is still mine. Now I must find Carlo—fix a date for the wedding.' Still mumbling incoherently, the woman walked out.

The horror, the tragedy of it all, all the wasted lives, brought tears to Marlene's eyes. As a young girl the Contessa had fallen in love with a married man, and because of status, pride—whatever one wanted to call it—she had blighted the lives of so many people. Marlene's own mother had married her cousin to give Marlene legitimacy, but she had only ever loved Paolo Rossi. Paolo's life had been blighted for years by a wife who cared nothing for him and would not let him touch her. Marlene remembered him telling her about a number of casual women in his life before he'd met her mother again and why he had needed them, but she had never quite believed him until now. And then there was Rocco, who had no relationship with his father to speak of . . .

She gasped. Rocco . . . 'Oh, my God!' Marlene exclaimed out loud, the sound echoing in the empty room. Caterina was his half-sister!

It was a very subdued Marlene who sat in the back of the car with Signor Toni on the drive back to Amalfi. Almost being caught by the Italian paparazzi as they had left the Rossi building had not helped her mood.

Signor Toni took her hand in his and squeezed it gently. 'Your father would have been proud of you today. You should be happy.'

She raised her eyes to his. 'I couldn't have done it without you. Thank you from the bottom of my heart,' she said sincerely, then added, 'But so much deceit is hard to comprehend.' A tear fell down her cheek, quickly followed by another, and when the old man put his arm around her to comfort her she found herself telling him all about her confrontation with the Contessa in the powder room. 'I can't believe such wickedness,' she ended, brushing the tears from her cheek.

'You are like your father. If he had a fault it was that he always looked for the good in people and sometimes missed the bad. I remember him as a young man, coming back from England for the first time. He came to tell me of the continuing success of our venture and that he had fallen in love with an English girl. He was happy and so full of life. Three weeks later he came back to tell me he was marrying the Contessa, and he would not explain why. Now I know... But you must not cry, my dear. Years later, when he had been reunited with your mother and he visited me again, I saw once more the happy young man of his youth.'

The car stopped outside Signor Toni's house, but he did not alight immediately. 'This week, meeting you and your brother has given me more pleasure than I can say. Don't let the Contessas of this world get to you. And come and see me again some time.' In a courtly gesture he lifted her hand to his lips and kissed it. 'Promise?' he said. And she did.

Drawing up outside the glass pyramid entrance of the villa, Marlene stifled a feeling of disgust. The quicker she got herself and her brother away from here the better, she thought.

After a quick, if rather late lunch with Paul, she said her goodbyes to Eta and, bundling her brother into the car, joined him on the back seat. It was a short drive to Rocco's home, and Marlene heaved a sigh of relief when Aldo stopped the car outside the entrance door. Ten minutes later she was standing in the bedroom Paul always used and looking down on his sleeping form.

The innocence of youth. He had crawled into bed to take a nap without a word of protest, after a promise that he could go swimming in the pool later. But Marlene felt restless, her mind a host of conflicting thoughts. Whether it had been wise to come to Rocco's home after all she had learnt that morning she was no longer sure. She debated calling a taxi and booking into a hotel for the night.

She sighed heavily and eased her feet out of the high-heeled shoes. Wise or not, she was too tired and too dispirited to start looking for a hotel for one night—no easy task at the height of summer and the tourist season. Suddenly the thought of returning to England in the morning seemed highly desirable.

Shrugging out of her jacket and skirt, she laid them at the foot of Paul's bed and, picking up the holdall that held their overnight needs, walked along to the bathroom. She felt dirty, contaminated by what she had learnt. In the context of human relationships, the story must rank as one of the biggest failures ever. Stripping naked, she got into the shower and turned on the spray. The plot would make a great Fellini-type film, she thought drily. It had everything—passion, deceit, betrayal, not to mention adultery. All it needed was incest... She stopped dead, turned off the water and got out of the shower. Her last thought had been too horrible to contemplate.

Quickly she picked up a towel and dried herself, then, taking her swimsuit from the holdall, she pulled it on. Not stopping, she hurried out and into the garden. She saw the swimming pool and dived in. She forced her tired body to swim length after length of the pool in a fast crawl, hoping to force the unwanted thought from her mind. But finally, breathless, she dragged herself out of the water and sank down on a nearby lounger.

She closed her eyes, but she could not close her mind. She saw once again Rocco in the herb garden with Caterina, saw the other woman caressing his chest. No, they couldn't have been lovers. She was becoming paranoid. Hadn't Rocco himself told her that he thought of Caterina almost like a sister? It was her over-fertile imagination. But a devilish voice inside her head whispered, Yes, but Rocco didn't *know* Caterina was his half-sister, did he?

The distant ringing of a telephone stopped her tortured thoughts, and, leaping to her feet, she dashed back inside to answer it.

The telephone was on an antique hand-painted table just inside the hall. She picked up the receiver and said breathlessly, *'Pronto.'*

'So you are there,' a deep masculine voice replied rather curtly. 'I wasn't sure you would be.'

'Yes—yes, I am,' Marlene said eagerly. The sound of Rocco's voice was somehow reassuring to her. 'Are you on your way?'

'Not exactly. Is Paul with you?'

'Well, yes, of course.' Just then she heard his little voice calling from the bedroom. 'In fact I think he's just woken up,' she said, with a smile in her voice.

'In that case I won't keep you. I rang to tell you I'll be late in getting back. I have a dinner engagement, so get yourselves something to eat, and, as you're probably tired after your busy day, go to bed.'

'Yes, all right,' Marlene said quietly. Even over the telephone she had recognised the drawling sarcasm in his tone. 'Is something wrong?' she could not help asking.

A cynical laugh echoed down the wire. 'Wrong? What could possibly be wrong, when I have a willing woman waiting for me and warming my bed? *Ciao.*' And he rang off.

Marlene shivered, and after replacing the receiver she rubbed her bare arms. Someone walking over my grave, she thought, and went to get Paul.

She spent the rest of the day with Paul in the pool, and when she finally persuaded him that it was time to go indoors she bathed him. Dressed in his nightclothes, he followed her into the kitchen. It was a cosy room. The pine units formed a galley-style kitchen that opened onto the breakfast area, where a round pine table stood surrounded by ladder-backed wood chairs. On one wall was a dresser, holding a collection of blue china that matched the plates standing all along the picture rail that trailed around the walls.

Marlene smiled when she discovered that the freezer and refrigerator were stocked to capacity with a multitude of pre-cooked pre-packed meals, all labelled and obviously prepared by Rocco's absent housekeeper. The man was certainly not going to starve, or cook...even if he did live on his own for months. Deciding on pasta in a rich cream and ham sauce, she set it to reheat and laid the table for Paul and herself.

The food was delicious, and with ice cream to follow made a perfect supper. By the time they had finished Paul's eyes were drooping, and Marlene picked him up to carry him to bed. She passed the suitcases standing in the hall, and worried again about the wisdom of staying here. Even now she could still call a cab and leave.

By ten o'clock at night, she was beginning to wish she had. Bathed and ready for bed, wearing an over-large white T-shirt—a relic from her student days—with a message emblazoned across it that 'Achieving starts with Believing', she was curled up on a large soft-cushioned sofa in the elegant but homely lounge. Marlene looked around her and asked herself for the hundredth time what she was doing here. Paul was sound asleep in the other half of the house, and she felt totally alone.

It had seemed so simple yesterday, when she had decided to take Rocco up on his offer, even though she had been disappointed in his lack of support. As it happened, she hadn't needed his support—she was more than capable of looking after her own affairs—but that was not the point. Rocco didn't know that. With a sigh, she realised she was being totally unreasonable. On the one hand she was a super-efficient business woman, but at the same time she wanted her lover to lean on . . . How mixed-up could one get?

She tipped her head back against the cushions and, unfurling her long legs, stretched. God, she was tired! Closing her eyes for a moment, she debated going to bed.

Somehow, even after all the intimacies she had shared with Rocco, she still did not feel comfortable with the idea of crawling into his bed on her own. Plus, she knew that she was going to have to tell Rocco about the morning's meeting before anyone else did. She yawned widely and her eyelids drooped. She was asleep.

She didn't hear the door or the man walking into the room. The first inkling she had that she was not alone was when, on opening her eyes, she saw Rocco towering over her.

'Sleeping the sleep of the innocent, were you?' he asked mockingly, his dark gaze taking in her rumpled state.

Marlene's hand reached up and, still drowsy, she stared at Rocco, her golden eyes wide with mingled surprise and love. 'You're back,' she murmured. But he didn't take her outstretched hand.

'As you see.'

She pulled herself up to a sitting position and smoothed the cotton shirt down to her knees. 'Did you have a good trip?' she asked rather stiltedly. Her glance took in his broad-shouldered form, elegantly clad in a lightweight cream suit and a tan shirt. But his tie and the first few buttons of his shirt were pulled loose, and he had a distinctly dishevelled air about him.

'Such touching concern,' he drawled, looking down at her with a mocking smile. 'I suppose I should be flattered.' He arched one black brow. 'Given your busy life and sudden wealth and notoriety.'

'Notoriety?' she queried, staring at him. Silently he quite casually removed his jacket and let it fall on the arm of the sofa. His tie followed, but she could sense the barely controlled tension in him, and she stiffened as he dropped down beside her on the sofa. 'What do you mean?' she asked with a sinking heart. Somehow he had already heard about her triumph of the morning.

'You looked very good on the television news this evening. Almost unrecognisable to some who know you.'

She gulped. 'The television?'

'Yes, and very interesting it was too. The Contessa had arranged for the Press to be on hand, hoping to reveal her plans for Rossi International. Instead they got an almost incoherent interview from her and a brief picture of you being handed gracefully into a Mercedes by Signor Toni. An old man who never looked sideways at a woman until you appeared.'

'Oh, no.'

'Oh, yes,' said Rocco, and his voice hardened as he went on, 'I was right about you from the first. Your capacity to bemuse older men must be inbred. But then why should I worry, as long as you warm my bed?' And, sliding an arm around her shoulders, he hauled her towards him.

Curved against his side, the familiar warmth of his big body enveloping her, Marlene should have felt relieved but the opposite was true. She tried to put some space between them, but his arm tightened around her back, his fingers digging into the skin under her arm. 'I can explain,' she said huskily.

'There is no need.' With his other hand he clasped her chin and turned her face towards his. 'I know everything. I have just spent a very enlightening evening dining with my father,' he drawled silkily. 'And surprise, surprise—the owner of a pleasant country herb garden turns out to be a financial wizard with her own company and an international client base.' His black eyes looked mockingly down at her. 'Now, for some women that would be enough. But not you, Marlene.'

She swallowed, her throat tightening. 'I had no choice...' she began to explain. 'I promised Paolo I would try and save his company. I couldn't tell you—you must see that.'

'I see nothing,' he ground out from between his teeth, 'except a mercenary little bitch who set out to make a fortune and a fool of me at the same time.'

Her temper flared at the unfairness of his comment, but still she tried to justify her behaviour. 'I couldn't tell you the truth because you were too close to the other people involved.'

'And I wasn't close to you?' he snarled, his black eyes flaring with controlled anger. 'You lay in my bed, in my arms. I had y—'

She cut him off. 'I thought you said never to mix business with pleasure,' she reminded him.

'Did I?' he snapped as he dragged her across his knees, his eyes leaping with fury and something else. 'More fool me,' he bit out, and his mouth crashed down on hers in a biting, savage kiss, forcing her lips apart.

She tried to push him away, her hands shoving against his chest, but he was too strong for her. He pushed her back so her head fell against the other arm of the sofa and she was splayed across him. Grasping her hands in one of his, he forced them over her head, and with his other hand across her stomach he held her immobile.

'Get off me!' she cried, her voice shaking with panic as she registered his furious expression.

'Very appropriate.' There was a derisory gleam in his eyes as he read the motto printed on her shirt. '"Achieving starts with Believing". You'd better *believe* I'm going to have you, Marlene—because I am definitely going to *achieve* it.' And his head bent to kiss her again.

She struggled beneath him, her body bucking, then somehow she was flat on her back and his whole weight was pinning her down. It wasn't supposed to be like this, she thought frantically, even as her lips involuntarily parted beneath the pressure of his kiss.

CHAPTER TEN

'PLEASE, ROCCO,' Marlene cried, and with her hands free again she pushed against his chest. 'Not like this.' His lower torso pressed hard against her, making her aware of his arousal, while he leant back slightly, his elbows either side of her shoulders, and stared down into her flushed face.

'"Please, Rocco,"' he mimicked savagely. 'What pity did you show to the Contessa? I was right about you the first time I saw you. You are a devious, lying, mercenary little bitch.' His black eyes glittered with fury. 'You couldn't be satisfied with a share in the Rossi empire for your half-brother. You had to have it all. Never mind about the man's legitimate wife and child, you had to grind their faces in it. And I thought I knew you. I actually considered asking you to ma—' He shook his black head. 'You made a complete fool out of me.'

'No, no...' Marlene said desperately, realising Rocco did not know the full story. 'I—' And she stopped. How could she tell him that Paolo Rossi was her father without telling him that Caterina was his half-sister? 'What about Caterina?' she asked, suddenly desperately needing to know. 'Was she ever your lover?'

'Jealousy, Marlene?' he exclaimed in furious disbelief, jumping to a totally erroneous assumption. 'Is that what goaded you on? Well, you need not have bothered. I've never laid a hand on Caterina.'

'No, I'm not jealous—you've got it all wrong,' she said frantically.

'Wrong? My God, I have!' Rocco said savagely, and his hands moved to tangle in her hair, allowing the whole

169

of his weight to fall on her. 'So much for your damn lies,' he snarled, his handsome face, contorted with rage, only inches from her own. '"I know nothing about business,"' he mimicked. 'Like hell you don't. You've been running rings around everyone since I picked you up at the airport.' He laughed cynically. 'But at least I got something out of it,' he said, and, stroking one hand down her neck, he cupped her breast through the fine cotton of her shirt. 'I got to use your luscious body— who cares about your black heart?'

Marlene's breath caught in her throat at the insult, and she felt like crying at the injustice of it all. 'You don't understand—' She tried again, but his mouth clamped down on hers, kissing her with brutal aggression.

She struggled to get away, but he was too strong, too heavy. She tried to hit him, but in the tussle that ensued in one lightning movement he ripped her shirt over her head, and, catching her hands in one of his, wrenched them above her head again. Then he moved slightly, so she was trapped against the inside of the sofa.

'I understand all I need to,' he sneered, his hand stroking down over her naked body, shaping over her waist and hips. He thrust a muscular thigh between her long legs and moved against her in a parody of the sex act. 'This is what you like—your reason for being here.'

Marlene drew a shuddering breath and gazed up at him, futilely searching his face for a sign of any kind of affection. But the implacable determination in his black eyes told her all too clearly what he intended. He wanted to possess her with his body, humiliate her as he thought she had humiliated him.

'You know you do,' he said silkily, his fingers trailing up over her waist to her breast and flicking the rosy tip. 'And who am I to disappoint you?' he taunted.

To Marlene's shame, her traitorous flesh responded instantly to his touch. Never mind that he hated her.

Never mind that he was simply using her. She could not disguise her need. And when he lowered his head, his mouth grazing over her aroused nipples, back and forward, she thought she would go mad with the effort to resist him.

'It's no good, Marlene,' he whispered against her breast. 'You want me.' He trailed kisses up her throat, and all the time his thigh moved rhythmically against her.

'Please—' she whimpered, not sure if she was asking him to stop or continue. But her plea was swallowed by his mouth covering hers.

If his kiss had been brutal again she might have held out. But, confusing her utterly, his mouth was gentle and his tongue circled her full lips, then probed the moist heat beyond. She closed her eyes and helplessly succumbed to the magic of his mouth, and when he finally let her hands go free she did not try to push him away, but reached for his head and plunged her fingers into his thick black hair.

She groaned her delight when he lifted his head and stared into her passion-glazed eyes, and then let his eyes sweep lower, over her naked form. Frantically she burrowed her hands up under his shirt, her fingers tracing muscle and sinew in feverish tactile pleasure.

'You are so luscious,' Rocco growled, and moved to suckle once more at her proud breasts.

She wasn't aware of the moment when he removed his clothes, but when he shifted slightly, sliding his hands beneath her and lifting her to meet the hard thrust of his manhood, she was aching for him. The blood coursed through her veins like quicksilver, igniting every nerve and fibre of her body. She was inflamed by the hard, pulsing heat of him to the very core of her being. She locked her long legs around his waist, her back arching up, urging him on. But Rocco had a different agenda.

'Softly, softly,' he rasped against the soft curve of her throat, his hand slipping between their linked bodies, his finger stroking the nub of her passion. Marlene trembled on the brink but he would not be hurried. Playing her like a maestro, he took her to the edge over and over again, until every nerve in her body was screaming for release.

'Please ... please,' she begged him, and he thrust hard and fast, and the climax hit them simultaneously, shattering in its intensity. Rocco collapsed on top of her, and for a while she floated in a mindless peace, the ragged sound of Rocco's breathing comforting to her ears. Then Rocco rolled off the sofa and stood up.

Her golden eyes soft with love, she watched as he pulled on his trousers. She knew she had a lot of explaining to do, but after the passion they had shared she was confident that this time Rocco would listen, and forgive her deception. But she was wrong ...

'You can sleep in the room next to your brother tonight, and I'll arrange for you both to get to the airport in the morning.' He glanced down at where she lay naked on the sofa. 'And cover yourself. I've had enough for one night,' he opined, with no trace of emotion. And when the shock of his words froze her into immobility he added, 'You understand? Or shall I spell it out for you?'

Marlene understood all too well. What she had become in the last hour was a one-night stand. She scrambled into her T-shirt and looked up at Rocco with anguished eyes, incapable of saying a word. Then suddenly, for a split second, she saw a flash of the same pain reflected in his eyes, and it gave her the will to make one lastditch attempt to explain. 'I don't know what your father told you, Rocco, but please let me try to explain—'

'Forget it, Marlene. It is over.' Turning, he walked away, flinging over his shoulder, 'Be packed and ready by eight. I don't want you in my home one minute longer than is necessary.'

Six weeks later, in the Johanson Herb Garden at two o'clock on a Monday afternoon, Marlene, with a basket on her arm, stopped by the rows of raspberry bushes and, reaching out, picked one of the juicy red fruits. She popped it into her mouth. They were ready for harvesting.

Methodically she worked between the rows, breathing in the clean fresh air and slowly filling the basket with fruit, glancing up now and then at the fluffy white clouds that drifted by, thinking how the change of seasons was coming. Soon it would be autumn, and soon she would have to make changes in her life.

She had got back from town half an hour ago, feeling restless and worried, and had changed into a pair of old blue jeans and a well-washed blue sweatshirt and headed for the garden. Now she hesitated and looked around her, and then down at the almost full basket, a sad smile on her face.

It seemed incredible that it had been in this spot, not even two months ago, that she had lain on the warm earth and watched Rocco Andretti stride down the garden. She dropped to her knees and placed the basket on the dry earth. The day itself was quite warm, with a gentle breeze rustling the leaves. Not unlike that first day, she thought, wriggling into a sitting position. She clasped her hands around her bent legs and rested her chin on her knees. Paul had gone back to school today, for the start of the autumn term, and she was alone. Alone with her thoughts... and with a hard decision to make. Should she contact Rocco Andretti again or not?

She closed her eyes and relived her disastrous last night in Italy. She shivered, but not with the cold. When she had finally picked herself up off the sofa and gone to the guest room, she had not slept a wink. At seven the next morning she had been ready to leave, with Paul dressed and waiting. She had been in the process of telephoning for a taxi when a cold-eyed, grim-faced Rocco had appeared. He had insisted on escorting them to the airport. The memory of the icy contempt in his eyes when he had left them standing in the departure lounge still had the power to make her shudder...

Opening her eyes, Marlene sighed. What was the use of reliving the past? She had cried all the tears she was going to for Rocco Andretti. The first week she'd been home she had done little else. But not any more. She took a deep breath. It would never have worked anyway. Who was it who had said, 'O what a tangled web we weave, When first we practise to deceive!' or words to that effect? she thought wryly. There had been far too much deceit, and too many secrets within secrets, for a relationship between herself and Rocco to stand any chance...

Picking up the basket, Marlene got to her feet, her mind made up. She had a good career, a good life, an adorable brother. It might be a small family but it was a loving one, and as for contacting Rocco again—when hell froze over sprang to mind...

The decision made, Marlene, head bent, attacked the fruit bushes with grim determination. The raspberries were not for sale; there were not enough of them. Usually she simply froze them and made the odd pie, but suddenly she had a craving for raspberry jam. There must be a recipe in one of the cookbooks her mother had been so fond of collecting, she mused as she neared the end of a row, and, lost in her own thoughts, she failed to hear the footsteps this time. She didn't realise she was not alone until she lifted her head.

'Hello, Marlene.'

The basket dropped from her nerveless fingers, scattering the fruit all over the ground. 'Rocco,' she whispered, amazed, as she looked at him.

He was standing in front of her, his tanned face seeming thinner and slightly pale. But his wide-legged stance, the large hands hooked into the pockets of well-cut denim jeans that clung to his muscular thighs and lean hips, the checked wool shirt emphasising his broad shoulders—all these reinforced the impression of a powerful, aggressive male.

Marlene took a step back and moistened her dry lips with her tongue. 'What are you doing here?' she demanded.

'I came for you.' He took a step towards her.

She stiffened. She caught the scent of his cologne—he was much too close—and she made to step back again. His hand reached out and caught her arm, and she tensed involuntarily.

'Marlene—the basket.' He glanced down at the ground and she followed his gaze. She had almost tripped backwards over it.

'Oh,' she murmured, brushing away his hand and stepping sideways. 'Well, as you can see I was busy, and it's your fault I dropped the fruit,' she said without preamble. 'So I suggest you take yourself off and let me get on with my work.'

'I know it's my fault, Marlene,' he replied, his voice clipped. 'Everything that has happened between us is my fault. I realise that now.'

Had she heard him right? Or were her ears playing tricks on her? She looked up into his eyes and there was no mistaking the sincerity in his dark gaze.

He jammed his hands back into his pockets as though he was afraid he would reach out to her if he didn't. 'Surprised?' he asked shortly. 'That I finally got over my arrogance, my raging hormones long enough to listen to the truth and now I want to apologise?'

'The truth?' Her lip curled. 'The truth according to your father and the Contessa.' She eyed him bitterly. 'No, thanks,' she said tightly, and, kneeling down, she picked up the basket and began gathering the fallen fruit. She could not bear to look at him; he was out of her life and that was the way she wanted it. But that didn't stop her pulse quickening when he dropped to his knees beside her and grasped her hand on the basket.

'Leave the damn fruit and listen to me.'

She eyed him scathingly, her temper rising. How dared Rocco walk back into her life just when she had decided to blot him out for good? 'Why the hell should I? You wouldn't listen to me, and now it's too late.'

He smiled—a grim twist of his lips. 'Because I love you.'

Marlene froze in the act of picking up a raspberry. Were her ears deceiving her yet again? He moved closer—so close that she had to look straight into his face.

'I am on my knees. I will grovel in the dirt if I have to,' he ground out. 'But you must give me a chance. Listen to me.'

Her mouth fell open, her golden eyes wide and unblinking. One hand still hung in the air; the other had a death grip on the handle of the basket. She was not imagining it. He had said he loved her. That he would grovel if he had to. How many times in the past few weeks had she dreamt of just such a scenario? The arrogant, overbearing Rocco on his knees to her. And now he was... But dared she believe him?

'I do love you, Marlene,' he said in a deep, dark voice, his gaze holding hers, his handsome face taut with barely controlled emotion. 'I know you must find it hard to believe, but please...' He caught her wavering hand in his. 'Please let me try to explain.'

She wanted to cry. She remembered saying the same words to him, and being ignored.

His fingers tightened around her hand. 'Damn it, Marlene—say something.'

She glanced around the garden in a daze, and then lifted her eyes to his. 'I... I don't think...' She couldn't get her thoughts into any kind of order. He was kneeling in the dirt, looking at her as if she was all he had ever wanted.

'You don't need to think.' He reached his other arm around her back and caught her up against him, his arms enfolding her as his mouth found hers and took it in a wild, passionate kiss.

Her fingers tangled in his black hair of their own volition. It had been so long, and she ached for his touch. She moaned when he lifted his head to stare down into her flushed face.

'You still want me, Marlene,' he ground out. 'You can't deny it.' They were knee to knee on the dry earth, and she looked at him and sighed heavily. 'I never tried to. It was you that . . .' He had chased her away without a backward glance.

'Let's get something straight right now,' Rocco said roughly. 'I never wanted you to leave. It was pride, male ego—call it what you will—that made me behave like an arrogant, conceited jerk the last night we were together, and I will never forgive myself for the way I treated you. But can't we put it all behind us and start again?'

Marlene rested her hands on his broad shoulders. 'It's not possible,' she said, hanging onto her self-control by a thread. 'With all that has happened.'

'Anything is possible if you want it enough—and God knows I want you in my life more than anything in the world.'

Her eyes lingered on his handsome face and a tiny kernel of hope fluttered in her heart. He looked sincere, but . . . She pushed on his shoulders and stood up. 'We'd better go in the house,' she offered, glancing down into his upturned face, a wry smile twisting her full lips. 'Grovelling in the dirt really doesn't suit you.'

Rocco leapt to his feet and hauled her hard against his taut body. 'For you—anything,' he declared, and brushed his lips against hers.

She wriggled out of his arms, wishing it were that simple. Kiss and make up. But there had been too much hurt and heartache. He could still seduce her with a touch, a smile—the chemistry was as strong as ever. But she was wary now. He could also kill her with a single sentence—as she knew to her cost.

Marlene suddenly felt terribly nervous. Rocco was sprawled on the sofa in her living room, his long legs stretched out, the pale sun shining through the mullioned windows etching the harsh contours of his face, and she realised he looked exhausted. 'Would you like a drink? Coffee?'

Rocco shook his black head. 'Come and sit down,' he drawled, his eyes narrowing on her. 'I have to talk to you.'

Marlene swallowed, her pulse rate rising, but she did as he said and gingerly sat down on the edge of the sofa.

'I can't blame you for being wary,' he said quietly. 'The last time we were on a sofa together I virtually raped you.'

'No,' she denied vehemently. 'It was never that.'

'Wasn't it?' Rocco cast her a sidelong glance. 'Thank you for that, Marlene, but I still feel an absolute heel. You see, I had dined with my father, at his command, and of course he gave me a very edited version of the result of your morning's work. I was stunned to discover you were a financial wizard, and from there it was quite easy to believe you were a totally mercenary golddigger—the poor Contessa outsmarted by a slip of an Englishwoman. But what angered me most was the realisation that I had asked you to trust me and you quite obviously hadn't. I had it all worked out—I went to Rome for informal talks with the chancellor of University College London, who was holidaying there. I agreed to spend the next year in London.'

Marlene's mouth fell open, her eyes wide with amazement as he continued, 'I saw you and I—and Paul, of course—living here during term-time and vacationing in Amalfi. I had it all organised and I was coming back to ask you to marry me, conceitedly believing your answer was a foregone conclusion—'

'I remember you almost said so,' Marlene cut in, recalling his bitten-off statement that fatal night. If what he said was true he had actually arranged his life around her, and her heart expanded with joy at the knowledge. When he had left for Rome he had told her to be waiting for him, had told her they were going to celebrate, but she had been too angry and resentful at his leaving to take any notice.

Rocco had cared about her. Still did... And but for her own folly they would have been engaged by now. 'Rocco.' She whispered his name, but he stopped her with a finger to her lips.

'Please, Marlene, don't say anything. Let me finish. My pride took a heavy battering that night. I bitterly resented the way you had turned me into a lovesick fool, and I was furious because I realised you didn't love me. How could you when you didn't trust me?' The look he gave her was full of self-mockery. 'I now know your reasons, but at the time I simply wanted to hurt you as I was hurting.'

Marlene instinctively reached out and put her hand on his thigh. 'No, Rocco, it wasn't your fault. I wanted to tell you the whole truth. I did try once, but...' her golden eyes smiled up into his '...that was just after the first time we made love, and after that I didn't dare in case you turned against me. Our relationship was so new. I didn't want anything to spoil it. I was a coward.'

Rocco's hand covered hers on his thigh and his dark eyes burnt down into hers. 'Is that the truth?' he demanded hardily.

Taking her courage in both hands, she told him how she felt. 'Yes. You told me yourself you were not looking for a wife, just a lover, and I had no experience in that kind of relationship. I had only ever had one serious boyfriend and we only...' Fighting down the colour in her face, she determinedly carried on. 'We only did it once. Then I discovered he was picking my brains to get a partnership in the firm where we both worked instead of me.'

'The bastard!' Rocco exclaimed, angry on her behalf, and pulled her to his side so she rested in the curve of his arm. With his other hand tipping her chin, he added, 'Tell me who it was and I'll kill him.'

Marlene had to smile. 'That's exactly what Paolo said. But you can see why I was afraid to tell you the truth. My faith in the male sex was badly dented. And though I love you, and wanted to believe in you, I was...' She got no further as his mouth crashed down on hers.

A long moment later she stared up at him breathlessly. 'What was that for?'

'I love you, Marlene, and a moment ago you said you loved me. Did you mean it?' Rocco demanded, lifting his hand to stroke her burning cheek.

'I...I...' She hadn't realised she had given herself away so thoroughly.

'God! Don't go coy on me now, Marlene. I have to know.'

'Yes, I loved you,' she murmured, hypnotised by the expression in his eyes.

'Past tense,' he said, and, drawing her head to his, he rubbed his lips softly on hers, mouthing gently, 'You loved me once, Marlene. Let me try and make you love me again.'

For long moments there was silence, until Marlene needed to breathe or die from his kiss, and, leaning back in his arms, she said breathlessly, 'You don't need to try—I do love you.'

When he would have kissed her again, she held him back with a hand on his chest. 'But is love enough?' It was so easy to forget all that had happened in the past now she was held in his arms, but they had to talk—get rid of all secrets. 'It's six weeks since I left Italy. What made you change your mind about me now? Surely not your father?'

'The six longest weeks of my life.' Rocco husked, and, pushing her against the back of the sofa, he lowered his head.

'No,' said Marlene. It was too easy to fall into his arms with an avowal of love. She needed answers, needed to be able to trust him—now more than ever...

'OK, we have to talk. But I could think of better things to do.' Rocco grinned wryly. Half turning to face her, he squeezed her shoulder and, picking up her hand with his free one, laced her fingers with his. He looked down at their clasped hands for a second, then back to her lovely face.

'The reason it took me six weeks to get in touch with you does me no credit. When you first left I told myself I was well rid of you. I locked myself away in my house and drank myself into a stupor most nights, avoiding everyone. It was only when I finally went into Amalfi ten days ago and bumped into Signor Toni I realised what a fool I had been. I was going to ignore the man, but he wouldn't let me. He insisted on taking me for a drink and telling me the whole story. At first I didn't believe him.'

'You spoke to Signor Toni?' Marlene exclaimed.

'Yes, and when I left him I went straight to Naples and my father's house. After a rather drunken argument with my father—during which I learnt, by the way, that the Contessa has been admitted to a clinic for the mentally ill—I realised Signor Toni had been telling the truth, and the enormity of how badly you and your family had been treated sickened me to my soul.

'I know my own father betrayed the trust and good nature of his supposed best friend Rossi, and in doing so betrayed your mother. I know you are as much Rossi's daughter as Paul is his son. I know you set out to save your father's name, and I can't blame you for not trusting me with your true purpose. In fact I am amazed and thankful you let me anywhere near you with a name like Andretti.

'The apology hasn't yet been invented that can tell you how sorry I am at the way my family has behaved towards you and yours. But I swear I will do everything in my power to make sure no one ever hurts, deceives or insults you ever again.'

Marlene stirred restlessly against his side. She believed his declaration and his apology, but she still had one last worry. 'Caterina—' she began.

'I know now why you asked me if I had ever made love to Caterina,' he cut in, his dark eyes narrowing, his expression grim. 'She is my half-sister, and for that reason alone I could hate my father. He should have told me—especially once the girl was older. It was pure luck that nothing happened. But then again, maybe there is something in the genes. I always thought of her more as a kid sister than a woman, in any case.'

'I am sorry,' she said softly. It must be hard for a man like Rocco to know that his own father had been deceiving him all these years.

'There is no need. I think in the back of my mind I have always had a suspicion. I told you once that as a young boy I discovered my mother in tears, and if I am honest I have never liked my father since. I used to feel guilty about it, but as I got older I realised you can love people because they are your parents, but it does not necessarily follow that you have to like them. My father always had a mistress—dozens over the years.'

'The Contessa said the other women were just a smokescreen so no one would realise they were having an affair,' Marlene interjected.

Rocco threw back his head and laughed out loud. 'My God, the woman really was deluded if she believed that. My father only ever had one goal in his life: to be wealthy and enjoy himself. He married my mother for her money and I was the requisite son to carry on his name. But in all honesty he was never a father to me. Paolo Rossi spent more time with me when I was a child than my father ever did.

'I don't know why I imagined our relationship would change after the death of my mother. Perhaps I felt guilty, as she left me her personal fortune. When I came back from South Africa I had the stupid idea of making it up with my father and splitting my inheritance—hence my attempt to help him by coming to England and meeting you.' He glanced sideways at her. 'That is the only favour he has ever done for me. He gave me the chance to meet you again.'

'And you hated me on sight,' she said.

Rocco lifted their clasped hands to his mouth and his brilliant white teeth nipped the back of her hand. 'I never hated you. I lusted after you. God, how I lusted after you. I didn't know what had hit me.'

She flushed slightly. 'Lust isn't love,' she said bravely.

He studied her lovely face with dark, intent eyes. 'I know—I was a fool. I was blinded by lust; I couldn't see past your luscious body. Which is why I behaved like a complete jackass.'

'And now?' Marlene dared to ask. 'Now you know the difference?' She still needed reassurance that he really did love her.

'Never doubt that I love you, Marlene,' Rocco replied, and, putting their joined hands against his chest so she could feel the heavy pounding of his heart, his expression deadly serious, he stared into her eyes. 'I think

I have always loved you from the first time I saw you, but at the time I didn't believe in love.' One dark brow arched sardonically. 'Given my father and friends, it is not so surprising.'

'You asked me to be your mistress,' she couldn't help inserting.

'That was when I thought you had been Paolo's mistress—and you didn't disillusion me,' he chided gently.

Guilt made her blush. 'I was stupid.'

'No, you were only trying to protect your brother. Something else I love about you. When I discovered the truth from the Contessa I was angry, but on the Sunday after we made love for the first time I had great difficulty hanging onto my anger. By the Monday, when you walked into my house and into my bed, I had resolved to marry you. I decided no one else was ever going to have you but me, and the very next morning I set about making the arrangements. But—arrogantly—I still wasn't prepared to admit it was love.'

'So when...?' Marlene murmured, needing to know.

'The night I left you to go to Rome. I turned and looked back at you, with Paul in your arms, and I knew without any doubt or qualifications that I loved you and wanted you to be the mother of my children.'

It was what she had wanted to hear, and she had not the heart to deny him any longer. Overcome with emotion, she leant forward, slipping her arm around his back. 'Thank you, Rocco,' she breathed against his lips.

'No, I thank you, my darling,' he said, and, freeing her other hand, he hauled her hard against his chest, his lips nuzzling her neck and then her ear. 'When did you know you loved me?' he murmured, and she realised Rocco was just as insecure as she had been.

Tilting back her head, a beautiful smile illuminating her face, she said casually, 'Well, it all started when I was grovelling in the dirt, weeding between the raspberry bushes, and I glimpsed this incredibly attractive man.'

'Seriously, Marlene.' He stopped her, his dark eyes soft and oddly vulnerable.

She raised one slender hand and gently traced the outline of his brow. 'I am serious. I took one look and I wanted you. Nothing like that had ever happened to me before, and after the first day in Italy I knew I loved you and always would,' she whispered softly, and pressed a soft kiss to his firm lips.

Rocco turned her in his arms, lifting her over his legs, and they kissed as they had never kissed before—openly, with love and tenderness, need and passion. Then he lifted his head and stared down at her flushed face, her lovely swollen lips, and said, 'You will marry me, Marlene? I won't insist you take my name—under the circumstances, you can keep your own—but marry me, and I solemnly swear I will look after you and Paul always and for ever.'

Marlene could have wept for her proud, arrogant lover. She knew what it must have cost him to say that she could keep her own name, and with equal generosity she responded, 'Yes, I will marry you, and I will be proud to be known as Mrs Rocco Andretti.'

For a long time there was only the occasional groan and whimper to break the silence in the sun-washed room.

'This is no good. I refuse to make love to my fiancée for the first time on a sofa,' Rocco rasped finally, sitting up and brushing back his thick black hair, his usual arrogance returning. 'Where is Paul?'

'At school. He'll be back at four.'

Rocco glanced briefly at the thin gold watch on his wrist, and then without a word he swung Marlene up in his arms and stood up. 'Show me the way to the bedroom, sweetheart.'

'I seem to remember you saying that once before and getting a bowl of fruit thrown at you.' Marlene chuckled, lacing her hands behind his neck.

Rocco stopped, an arrested expression on his handsome face. 'Which reminds me—what were you doing picking raspberries? Not the usual occupation of a financial consultant on a Monday, surely?'

'What about love in the afternoon?' she mocked lightly. 'You're going to take me to bed. Mind you, I'm no lightweight, and carrying me upstairs is a lot harder than along a hall.'

'In my present state, please don't mention hard,' Rocco growled. 'I need the exercise to stop me from exploding here and now...'

Marlene yawned widely, snuggled up against Rocco's huge, warm body spoon-fashion under the rose cotton sheet, with his large hand splayed across her stomach. She had never been happier.

'Tired, darling?' His deep voice feathered her shoulder, and his hand stroked from her stomach to cup her breast.

Turning around, she looked up at him with eyes full of love. 'Never too tired for you.' She grinned, but before Rocco could capture her mouth she stopped him. 'One little boy will be back very soon.'

'Damn.' Rocco grimaced. 'Foiled again.'

'Do you mind about Paul?' It suddenly hit Marlene that not every man would want to marry a woman with an almost four-year-old child to look after.

'God, no,' he declared, and, rolling over onto his back, he pulled Marlene on top of him. 'Don't ever think that. I love the little boy as much as I would love one of my own.' And, pulling her head down, he kissed her with passion and promise.

Lying on top of him, Marlene was aware of the re-newed stirring of his arousal, and she moved her hips against his hard thighs teasingly. She would have loved to give in to the sensual delight he promised, but he had reminded her of a more urgent problem. Rolling off him, she sat up. 'You asked me before why I was picking the raspberries', she reminded him.

'I don't care.' He slanted her a smug grin from where he lay flat on his back, his hands behind his head, looking like one incredibly satisfied, sexy male. 'Come back here and finish what you started.'

'No. Not until I've answered your question. You did say we had to be honest with each other,' she stated with mock humility, giving him a sly grin. 'I was picking raspberries because I had a sudden desire to make raspberry jam. In fact,' she mused as her stomach suddenly made a distinct grumbling noise, 'I'm hungry now. A cheese, cucumber and raspberry jam sandwich would go down a treat.'

'A *what*?' Rocco pulled himself up to a sitting position. 'The English are not renowned for their food, but that sounds disgusting.'

'Well, if you will assault a lady on a sofa totally unprepared...' She knew the exact moment she had conceived—their last night together in Italy. 'You might expect that six weeks later she'll have a few odd crav—' She didn't finish.

'My God! You're pregnant!' His arm curved around her shoulders, pulling her towards him, and, twisting his hand in her long hair, holding her face only inches from his, he demanded, 'Would you have told me if...?'

Marlene looked deep into his eyes and saw her own reflection and her own doubts mirrored there. 'Yes,' she said. 'But I only found out today.' She thought of her visit to the doctor, and her restlessness on her return, which had led her out into the garden. She recalled her decision not to contact him until hell froze over, and then Rocco's sudden appearance.

'I believe you because I need to. I feel bad enough that our child was conceived in anger. I couldn't stand the thought that you might never have told me as well.'

'Never say that. Our child was *not* conceived in anger. It might have started that way, but it certainly didn't end that way, as I recall. And I would have told you about the baby,' she reiterated firmly, and, closing the space between them, she pressed her lips to his, putting all her love and reassurance into the kiss.

He lifted his head and smiled down into her wide golden eyes. 'Thank you for that, Marlene. There have been enough lies between us already to last a lifetime—but never again.' Cradling her head with his hand, he breathed against her mouth, 'Our child—I never thought life could be so perfect.'

Marlene lifted her arms around his neck, a secret smile on her flushed face. They still had a lot of sorting out to do, a lot of adjustments to make, but time and love were on their side. Anyway, she told herself, crossing her fingers behind his head, it wasn't a lie. It was a miracle! Her private hell *had* frozen over... She was back in her lover's arms to stay...

HARLEQUIN WOMEN KNOW ROMANCE WHEN THEY SEE IT.

And they'll see it on **ROMANCE CLASSICS**, the new 24-hour TV channel devoted to romantic movies and original programs like the special **Romantically Speaking—Harlequin™ Goes Prime Time**.

Romantically Speaking—Harlequin™ Goes Prime Time introduces you to many of your favorite romance authors in a program developed exclusively for Harlequin® readers.

Watch for **Romantically Speaking—Harlequin™ Goes Prime Time** beginning in the summer of 1997.

If you're not receiving ROMANCE CLASSICS,
call your local cable operator or satellite provider and
ask for it today!

Escape to the network of your dreams.

See Ingrid Bergman and Gregory Peck in *Spellbound* on Romance Classics.

Take 4 bestselling love stories FREE

Plus get a FREE surprise gift!

Special Limited-time Offer

Mail to Harlequin Reader Service®

> **3010 Walden Avenue**
> **P.O. Box 1867**
> **Buffalo, N.Y. 14240-1867**

YES! Please send me 4 free Harlequin Presents® novels and my free surprise gift. Then send me 6 brand-new novels every month, which I will receive months before they appear in bookstores. Bill me at the low price of $2.90 each plus 25¢ delivery and applicable sales tax, if any*. That's the complete price and a savings of over 10% off the cover prices—quite a bargain! I understand that accepting the books and gift places me under no obligation ever to buy any books. I can always return a shipment and cancel at any time. Even if I never buy another book from Harlequin, the 4 free books and the surprise gift are mine to keep forever.

106 BPA A3UL

Name	(PLEASE PRINT)	
Address	Apt. No.	
City	State	Zip

This offer is limited to one order per household and not valid to present Harlequin Presents® subscribers. *Terms and prices are subject to change without notice. Sales tax applicable in N.Y.

UPRES-696   ©1990 Harlequin Enterprises Limited

The SECRETS WITHIN

The most unforgettable Australian saga since Colleen McCullough's *The Thorn Birds*

Eleanor—with invincible strength and ruthless determination she built Australia's Hunter Valley vineyards into an empire.

Tamara—the unloved child of ambition, a catalyst in a plan to destroy her own mother.

Rory—driven by shattered illusions and desires, he becomes a willing conspirator.

Louise—married to Rory, she will bargain with the devil for a chance at ultimate power.

Irene—dark and deadly, she turns fanatical dreams into reality.

Now Eleanor is dying, and in one final, vengeful act she wages a war on a battlefield she created— and with a family she was driven to control....

EMMA DARCY

Available in October 1997 at your favorite retail outlet.

 MIRA **The brightest star in women's fiction**

With a Free Gift proof-of-purchase
from any Harlequin® book, you can receive
a beautiful cubic zirconia pendant.

This stunning marquise-shaped stone is a genuine cubic
zirconia—accented by an 18" gold tone necklace.
(Approximate retail value $19.95)

Send for yours today...
compliments of HARLEQUIN®

To receive your free gift, a cubic zirconia pendant, send us one original proof-of-purchase, photocopies not accepted, from the back of any Harlequin Romance®, Harlequin Presents®, Harlequin Temptation®, Harlequin Superromance®, Harlequin Intrigue®, Harlequin American Romance®, or Harlequin Historicals® title available at your favorite retail outlet, together with the Free Gift Certificate, plus a check or money order for $1.65 U.S./$2.15 CAN. (do not send cash) to cover postage and handling, payable to Harlequin Free Gift Offer. We will send you the specified gift. Allow 6 to 8 weeks for delivery. Offer good until December 31, 1997, or while quantities last. Offer valid in the U.S. and Canada only.

Free Gift Certificate

Name: _____

Address: _____

City: _____ State/Province: _____ Zip/Postal Code: _____

Mail this certificate, one proof-of-purchase and a check or money order for postage and handling to: HARLEQUIN FREE GIFT OFFER 1997. In the U.S.: 3010 Walden Avenue, P.O. Box 9071, Buffalo NY 14269-9057. In Canada: P.O. Box 604, Fort Erie, Ontario L2Z 5X3.

FREE GIFT OFFER   084-KEZ

ONE PROOF-OF-PURCHASE
To collect your fabulous FREE GIFT, a cubic zirconia pendant, you must include this original proof-of-purchase for each gift with the properly completed Free Gift Certificate.

084-KEZR